PATRICIA HERMES

Sweet By and By

HARPERCOLLINS*PUBLISHERS*

Library of Congress Cataloging-in-Publication Data

Hermes, Patricia.

Sweet by and by / by Patricia Hermes.

p. cm.

Summary: Eleven-year-old Blessing has lived with her grandmother in a cabin in the
Tennessee mountains since she was two years old, secure in a relationship of love and
shared music, but now she has to accept that her grandmother is dying and that she
must continue life without her in a new home.

ISBN 0-380-97452-5 — ISBN 0-06-029557-0 (lib. bdg.)

[1. Grandmothers—Fiction.   2. Death—Fiction.   3. Mountain life—Tennessee—
Fiction.   4. Music—Fiction.   5. Tennessee—Fiction.   6. World War, 1939–1945—
Tennessee—Fiction.]   I. Title.

PZ7.H4317 Sw   2002   2001051452
[Fic]—dc21   CIP
                                                                        AC

Typography by Amy Ryan

1   2   3   4   5   6   7   8   9   10

❖

First Edition

For Elizabeth Mary Nastu

Sweet By and By

1

"Tell me about the snowstorm," I said.

"What snowstorm?" Monnie asked.

"You know what snowstorm," I said. "Tell me about my mama. Tell me again how I got to be named Blessing."

"Your mama named you Blessing 'cause you was such a blessing to her, coming after your papa had just died, and I've told you this about three thousand times."

"Tell me again," I said. "Tell about me as a baby."

"You didn't have no hair," Monnie answered. "You was bald as that stone over there till you were more'n a year old." She nodded her head at a large white boulder at the edge of the garden. She turned and squinted up her eyes at me. "Now why're you thinking about them old things?"

I shrugged, but I didn't answer. More and more lately, this had been happening to me. I'd be thinking of Monnie, and suddenly, I'd be thinking about my mama. Then, before I knew it, I'd find that the words had jumped out of my mouth and were hanging in the air between us.

Monnie bent to her hoe again, chopping at the hard earth, lines of sweat streaking her huge back and broad shoulders, shoulders almost as big as a man's. Her head was wrapped in a scarf, and from the back, it might have made you laugh—a man wearing a head scarf and a skirt and apron. But when you got to look at her up close from the front, there was no doubt Monnie was a woman. Just a big one.

"How come you're thinking about your mama so much these days?" she asked, breathing hard.

"No reason," I said. "I guess I was just thinking about snow. Maybe it'll snow again tonight." Which of course was not what I was thinking about. But I couldn't tell Monnie that.

"Well, think about this here garden," Monnie said. "We got to get this ground softened up and ready or we won't have no vegetables come summer. I don't see you breaking up them clods much."

I sighed. "I'm doing it, I'm doing it," I said. I lifted my hoe and followed Monnie down the row, hacking at the hard ground. My back was about broken, but I knew I couldn't quit till Monnie was ready to quit. And though Monnie is old and sick, she can work harder in the garden than anyone I know.

"Did my mama help with the garden?" I asked. "I mean, when she was my age?"

"She helped with the garden and hated every minute of it, just like you," Monnie said. "Not that she was lazy or nothing. She just didn't fancy getting her hands dirty."

"I don't mind getting my hands dirty," I said.

"I know you don't," Monnie said. "But your mama, she wanted to keep her hands nice for the dulcimer."

Monnie got to the end of a row, stopped, and turned to me. She took a big blue handkerchief out of her apron pocket—the long apron she always wore in the garden—and buried her face in it, then ran it up one side of her neck and down the other. "Lord have mercy, it's hot for a cold day," she said.

I nodded. Here it was mid-March, and the air was cold, and it still snowed at night. But when you worked in the sun, it felt like July. It's always that way here in the shadows on Star Mountain. It's hot—and then it's cold. In the day, the sun can bake you till you feel yourself turning hot and all yeasty-like inside, like a loaf of bread rising in an oven. And then the sun slides down behind the mountain peaks, and it's colder than a grave digger's rear end.

Monnie looked at me, her eyes squinted up in that thoughtful way she has sometimes, head tilted to one side. "Now how come your mama's on your mind like this?" she said again. "That's at least the hundredth thing you've asked about her this week. And with her dead more'n nine years now."

"Since I was two years old," I said. I knew because I had been told the story so many times. *And she died in a snowstorm on the mountain—just like I was born in a snowstorm on the mountain—and when she was found, she was reaching out toward home. Toward me. Those snowstorms, they're some of those "God things" Monnie always talks about, how God has his plans.* But I didn't say any of that out loud.

"So why's she haunting you now?" Monnie asked again, like a dog with a bone, not letting go.

"No reason. I told you."

But Monnie, she's too smart for that. She kept looking at me. "I ain't going nowhere," she said softly.

"I know that!" I said. But I was lying. And I had to look away. Because you can't lie and look Monnie straight in the face. You just can't. For some reason, I was scared lately—scared that Monnie would up and die, just like everybody else had. My papa had died in a mine accident the same day as my grampa, both of them together, before I even got born. And then two years later, my mama had died, too.

I still couldn't look at Monnie, but I could feel her eyes on me, studying me.

"How about this?" she said softly, after a few minutes had gone by. "How 'bout we get on down to Ellie's tonight? After we clean ourselves up some. You'd like that?"

"Yes!" I said.

"Good. Then let's get this garden done with," Monnie said, and she turned and started with the hoe again, working with a vengeance.

I followed her down the row, feeling more energy just knowing we were going to Ellie's. Some town folks might call Ellie's a restaurant. But it's not. It's just Ellie's, six tables on the porch with some chairs bunched around them and a mess of squirrel stew or rabbit stew or collards, whatever she'd cooked up that day. If a person got there early enough, and the places at table hadn't been filled up, you got to sit down and eat.

I've never figured out how Ellie charges people, or even if she does. But each person who eats there plunks down a bill or a coin, whatever they can. And then, after dark settles in, and the places are cleared at table, that's the time I wait for. Because it's then that Monnie picks up her fiddle and plays.

It draws people like moths to a candle. They come from all around, out of the hollow, across the road, and they gather there in the dark. Sometimes the only thing you can see is eyes, like deer eyes shining in the light, and sometimes you see the light of a corn pipe. Monnie just taps her toe, and that fiddle zings out a toe-tapping tune. And then she'll play a worrisome tune, and the notes slither out sad and sorry-like. And sometimes, oh, Lord! she makes that fiddle sing. It's like there is a heart, a real heart inside its hole there in the middle. And then I sing, too. I'm not pretty, or all round and curvy, like some girls. But I do have a sweet voice, and when I sing—well, something happens to me. It's like I'm not just plain old normal me anymore. I'm different, almost like—well, I feel like I love the world so much I think I'll just burst. I think some of the people at Ellie's come just to hear me sing.

Monnie and I worked harder for a while, racing the setting sun. At last, Monnie straightened up and rubbed at her back. "Think that'll do it for today. Wonder what Ellie will have cooked up tonight."

"Squirrel, probably," I said. "There's zillions of them around this spring."

"Deer, too," Monnie said.

"You know I won't eat if it's deer," I said.

"Pure foolishness," Monnie said.

I just shrugged. I wasn't going to try to explain again that deer are too pretty, too sweet and delicate and winsome-looking to eat.

"You'll go hungry," Monnie said then. "Best carry along a sack of something just in case."

We started up to the house. At the door, we stopped, Monnie breathing hard, and we stepped out of our shoes, all muddy and stuck with clods of earth.

Inside, Monnie stopped to touch the fiddle that hung on the baker's rack by the fireplace, right next to my mama's old dulcimer. "We'll see what kinds of music are inside here tonight. See what she lets out."

Monnie always talks that way about the fiddle, as if it's a real person who has music stored up inside. She says she doesn't even really play the fiddle. She just tucks it under her chin and lets the music out.

"'Sweet By and By,'" I said. That's my favorite, sad and sweet and lonesome sounding, about loved ones meeting again in the sweet by and by. It pulls up a song from my own heart, maybe because Monnie has told me it was my mama's favorite.

Monnie looked again at the fiddle, frowning a little. "I believe she has 'Sweet By and By,'" she said. She began washing up, rubbing her hands with that old yellow lye soap she makes. She looked over at me. "You gonna sing tonight?" she asked.

"My mama sang, didn't she?" I said, and then I looked away real quick. Seems like I can't guard my thoughts or words at all anymore.

But Monnie didn't seem to care that I'd mentioned my mama again. Because she answered. "Like a nightingale," she said softly. "Played that dulcimer and sang like a nightingale. Sweetest thing you ever heard."

I took in a deep breath and smiled. "I'll sing."

2

Monnie says I sang before I could even talk—but I don't know if that's true. I only know that I love to sing, like when I'm out working in the garden, or sitting on the porch with Monnie, or even just walking out on the mountain. Or more formal times, like at church. Folks are always asking me to sing, though I have to say I always feel shy, at least at first. Now, I sat on Ellie's porch, waiting till the eating was done, waiting for the music. It turned out to be a long, long wait. Because the folks there can eat. And eat! Supper was squirrel, just like I thought it might be. There were biscuits and gravy and even grits and collards, a real feast. Me, I guess I don't love food the way some do. I mean, I like to eat, and I love bread, most especially the bread Monnie bakes, and butter, when we can get it. But I don't go hog-wild over food the way some here do.

Like the Cravens. They were there, eating so hard and so fast you'd think they never got food. Knowing how many little ones they've got, eight or ten or so, it's possible they don't get time to eat, not with having to scurry around, feeding all those mouths. They didn't have any of their passel of kids with them that night.

Two of the Boltons were there, Poppy and Mason, and they were shoveling in food, too, not saying a word. Poppy is silent and kind of fierce-looking, with bushy gray eyebrows that meet in a straight line across his forehead and a beard so long he can tuck it in his belt. His wife, Mason, is quiet like him, with clear, pale eyes that don't focus quite right. There's an old lady who lives with them, called Georgie, and a harmed kind of child called just Child, but Georgie and Child must have been left home this night.

Poppy looked up when he saw me watching him and nodded. I nodded back, remembering how when I was little, he scared me because of how fierce he looked. Yet every time I met him, Poppy would pull something out of his overalls pocket for me—a lollipop or a whistle he had made out of a willow branch. Everybody says Poppy has the biggest heart on the mountain. They say he goes round after dark, fixing things that need fixing for folks who can't do it on their own, planting gardens and keeping them free of weeds and bringing food to sick folks, just leaving it at their doorstep. Monnie says he and Mason do it that way because they're private folks. They don't want any fuss made about things.

Reverend Tucker was there, too, but not Mrs. Tucker. Everyone knows how sickly she is, though most people think her sickness is mostly just in her head. Still, each person asked after her kindly. I like Reverend Tucker, though I don't agree with a lot of what he tells us about God knowing and seeing everything and caring even about the little birds falling from the trees. If God cares so much, how come the world is so messed up, with a big war going on and people getting killed? Reverend Tucker loves to eat, so he's often at Ellie's since his wife isn't able to cook for him. And he does love music. On Sundays, and even on Wednesday nights, his tiny church perched on the side of the mountain just rings out with song.

Hector and Sally Martin were there, her belly all swollen up with baby, him acting protective and fussy. The way she ate, you could tell she was eating for two.

In the far corner of the porch was the Maren family, just six of them: Mama and Papa, and Big

Mama and Big Papa, and Uncle Winnie and Aunt Rosie. Their two boys, Hector and Hawkie, they'd gone off to the war just this past week. I heard Mama saying they was big and could take good care of themselves. But from the way she was twisting her fingers around, you could tell she was hurting something bad. And lastly came Ellie. Ellie is tall, taller than most men on the mountain, with a big lot of white hair that she wears in braids, twisted around her head like a crown. She's a healer, knows all about herbs and things. She nodded at me as she crossed the porch, then went and sat at the far corner table with the Marens, her tall white head seeming to tower over everyone else there, even sitting down.

No one spoke much through supper, just quiet eating, with the spring frogs just beginning to peep in the background. The air smelled of spring, and I even thought I caught a whiff of bear, like they'd already left their winter caves. There was a small breeze playing around, and the candles flickered. On one side of the porch, Ellie had a coal fire going, and there were some sticks burning in the chimney pot in the corner, so though the night was cold, the porch warmed up nicely.

I felt quiet inside, like maybe my worries about Monnie were just that—worries, not real things. She seemed good tonight, was even eating up real good.

And she had worked in the garden for the whole afternoon and walked all the way here tonight. Maybe her coughing and weakness were past now, just a bad spell that had taken her.

So the evening wore on, no one in a hurry to do anything but eat and chat and wait for the music. Finally, though, everyone seemed to have had enough, and the women began to clear. The men lit up their pipes and started talking low about this and that. I got up to help and told Monnie to just stay put. For once, she listened to me. So the tables got cleared, and Ellie tucked away whatever money had been left for her.

And then, after a bit, Monnie scraped her chair back from the table and picked up the fiddle case from the floor beside her. She laid it across her lap, took out the fiddle and bow, and began tuning up. As soon as she did, people began shifting around. Some pulled their chairs in a sort of circle, wanting to be closer. Some moved over by the railing where they could prop their feet. But as Monnie fiddled around with the bow, the chairs stopped scraping, and snatches of conversation faded away like little dying bits of flame. Monnie fiddled quietly for a while, and then slowly, bits of song began drifting out. At first, Monnie played just a snatch of this and that, nothing that you could really hold on to. I love it when she does that and you never know just what will come next, what song will slide out, but something always does. She went on like that, and folks began tapping their feet, and moving their heads. And then, real quiet-like, she slid into "Jesus, Sweet Lover of My Soul." It took me by surprise, because it's been some time since I heard that one, but then I thought maybe she did it for the reverend. And sure enough, after a minute or two, Reverend Tucker began to sing, his low, deep-down voice giving praise to the Lord, and nobody else joined in, maybe out of respect.

After that, Monnie did "The Old Churchyard," and there was more humming and murmuring and other voices joined with Reverend Tucker's. Then she picked up the beat and burst out with "Barbr'y Ellen" and then "Go Tell Aunt Rhody."

She went on a long while, and some people sang, and some hummed, and sometimes there was no sound but the fiddle and the toe tapping. Then Monnie began "Uncloudy Day," one of her favorites. She smiled and looked up at me, her eyebrows raised, a question in her eyes. I breathed deep and nodded. And then my voice slid out, soft and low, and I felt shy because the minute I started, all the other voices died away.

I sang through to the end, a bit scared at first, the

way I always feel when everyone goes silent, listening, and just my voice is hanging out there alone in the night. But then, like always, I got used to it, and I could even smile and sing. And then, slowly, Monnie slid into "Sweet By and By," and I forgot all about being shy, forgot about everything except the music.

In the sweet by and by,
we will meet on that beautiful shore.

The more verses Monnie played, the more I lifted up my voice. I sang to Monnie. I sang to the Marens and to the Boltons and to Reverend Tucker and the Cravens. I sang to Hector and Sally Martin, and I sang to their baby, too. I sang to Ellie and to the people gathered round, ones who had crept out from across the road, faces I couldn't see.

I sang to the stars, sang to the coyotes who were calling in the distance, and to the mountains and to everything. I stopped worrying about Monnie and about loneliness and about everything. I just sang.

3

Later, after we had walked home under the full moon and got ourselves into bed in our own rooms, I lay awake, staring out at the moon. Monnie was all right. She'd walked all the way to Ellie's and only had to stop a couple of times. And her music was the best it had been in a long time. She hadn't even stopped to breathe deep when she got into the fast tunes. She was able to strum and tap her feet and just keep right on going the whole night long. And I had sung.

I'd be lying, though, if I said I wasn't a little worried. I was. Monnie had had a coughing spell on the way home that went on so long, it scared me. But after she stopped coughing, she said it was just too much night air. So lying there, looking out at the stars, I looked on the bright side. Everything was fine, and it probably would keep on being fine. Monnie was sick, but not real sick. And she was old, so you could expect her to get sick some.

That's what I told myself, and I knew it was right.

I sighed deep then, inviting sleep. Even with my eyes closed, I could sense the light of the moon, so bright and full, could hear the rustle of the trees. The branches of the big old cottonwood scraped against my windowpane, a comforting sound. When I was little, that sound used to scare me, but now it's just sweet and familiar. An owl called from the woods and was answered by another owl so close he was maybe right in my cottonwood. *Hoot, who,* he called, *Hoot, who?* I drifted off, feeling myself sinking deep into the quilts, listening to the comforting scraping of the branches, the sighing of the wind in the treetops, the hooting of the owl.

But suddenly, I sat straight up in bed. Stupid owl! I banged my fist against the window. There was the rustle of wings and a rushing sound as the owl flew up in alarm. My heart was thumping hard, and I sat, glaring at the window. But it wasn't really the owl that had made me mad. The minute I had begun to drift off to sleep, the thoughts had come back, worrisome thoughts. Just because I wasn't guarding them, they came stealing back on the wings of a dumb old owl.

"Blessing?" Monnie called. "That you? You all right?"

"Fine," I called back.

"That old owl bothering you?" she called. "Chatty, ain't he?"

"Annoying," I said.

"Well, if you can't sleep, come on in," she said. "We can talk some."

"I'll sleep," I said. Because my worries were too high in my mind to go in there with Monnie. She's too sharp, too smart. She would know. "'Night," I called.

"'Night," she answered.

I settled down again, pulling a quilt high around my shoulders and squeezing my eyes shut. I lay there stiff, trying to feel myself sink down into the quilts again. But I couldn't. Sleep wouldn't come, and the sounds that were comforting before—the wind, the scraping of the branches—just made me lonesome now.

When I was small, and nights made me lonesome, I used to go into Monnie's room all the time. Those nights, Monnie would pull me right up alongside her, and we'd snug up in her bed. If the timing was right, we'd wait for moonrise, watch the moon creep over the mountain. We'd watch the moonlight slide up onto the windowsill, cross the floor, then settle itself like company on the chair. Monnie would tell stories, mountain stories about how bears own Star Mountain, own most of Tennessee, in fact, and how us people got to watch our step and not barge in on them. She taught me about owls, how they're always looking for prey, how owl pellets hold bones. It doesn't matter to an owl whether the bones came from a rabbit or a frog, it was all food to that old owl. She also told how old folks say an owl will sometimes call your name. And when he does, that means you're about to die soon. She told me how when she was young, rabbits were her most favorite things, not to eat, but to love. And when she found out they were food for people, and for owls, then she couldn't love them anymore.

I sat up in bed. "Monnie?" I called, real softly, in case she was asleep.

"I'm awake," she called back.

I got up and pulled a robe around myself, then padded through the kitchen and into Monnie's room. I was about to settle myself in the chair that the moon sits in, when Monnie said, "Come on," and in the moonlight, I could see her patting the bed.

I hesitated just a second. It had been a while since we'd snuggled up together in bed, I guess because I'd been feeling too grown-up lately. But it was cold in the room, and I knew Monnie's bed would be warm and comfy. So I crossed the room and climbed into bed, pulling a quilt high around my chin.

"That's the way," Monnie said.

I leaned in close to her, my head against her shoulder.

"That's better," Monnie said, reaching out and cupping my chin in her hand for just a moment before letting go and tucking her hands under the quilt, too.

We were quiet for a long while, and I began to feel warm and sleepy again.

"Music was good tonight," Monnie said.

"Hmm," I answered.

"You sang real pretty. You sing prettier each time."

"Tell me about the day you learned to play the fiddle," I said, though I had heard the story a thousand times before.

"I didn't learn. It just happened. See, there was always music everywhere. When I was just a porch baby, I'd sit and listen to my daddy with his fiddle, my mama with the dulcimer. And when I got a little bigger . . ."

"But you were still just a yard baby," I said.

"Was still just a yard baby," she said. "One night I picked up that dulcimer. I lay it across my lap, picked up the noter, strummed a bit, and then . . ."

"And then the music just poured out!" I said.

I knew it wasn't that way. But I wanted her to tell it.

"Nooo," she said. "Nothing comed out. Just

squeaks and squawks, like a chicken on killing day. So then I picked up the fiddle. My daddy tucked it up tight against my chin, showed me how to hold the bow and . . ."

"And?" I said, still knowing, but so happy to be hearing the story again.

"And music just poured out," Monnie said. "I didn't do it, true as can be. It just happened. And that's how I know that music is stored up there inside. Even today, I just cradle it, hold it to me like a sweet child, bow it, and . . . it just sings itself out."

"Is that how my mama learned?" I asked, though I had heard this part of the story often, too.

"Sure is. She called up tunes on the dulcimer and the fiddle, too, done that when she was littler than you."

"I'm like you," I said. "When I touch the dulcimer, it just squawks. I'd rather sing."

"Why not?" Monnie said. "God blessed you with a voice. It's even sweeter than your mama's was. She had tone. But you got heart."

"Heart?" I said.

"Heart," Monnie answered. "Real heart. I can hear your heart in your voice."

"What's that mean?" I said.

"Oh, I don't know," Monnie said, and suddenly she sounded tired and even irritable, and I thought it best not to ask more. I wondered if Monnie could hear the worry in my heart. Was that too silly to think? You can't really know what someone is thinking because of how they sing, can you?

Monnie was breathing deep then, slow and sleepy, and I felt myself drifting off, sinking into the quilts. I thought about getting up and going back to my own bed, but this was so sweet, so warm.

"Every day," Monnie whispered, "every single day."

"Every day, what?" I asked.

But Monnie was asleep, breathing deep, her breath puffing in and out, in and out. And I was too warm and sleepy to go back to my own bed.

And then, after I don't know how long, maybe minutes, maybe an hour, suddenly, we weren't sleeping anymore. Monnie was coughing. She sat up in bed, struggling for breath, coughing that rough cough that has been roiling her for months and months now. She coughed and coughed, like her chest and lungs would split right open—or like she wanted them to split open to let in some air.

I sat straight up. "Monnie?" I said.

She just waved a hand at me, shook her head. And coughed. And coughed.

I scrambled up onto my knees and then leaned over her. I had learned to do this months ago, when she first started getting so sick. I pulled her forward, then took her arms and pulled them up high over her head. She says it helps, makes her lungs stretch and let in more air.

But this time, she fought me off, gasping, gasping, her head rolling frantically, her eyes wide like a deer's caught in a trapper's light. She was dying, I knew it. And I wasn't going to let her die!

"Monnie!" I said. "Monnie?" I was just ready to start beating on her chest, her back, anything, when just as sudden as it came on, the coughing stopped, or almost stopped. She waved a hand again, patting the air, like she was saying, Hold on, hold on. But she was still gasping, her breath still raggedy in her throat, her eyes still wide and scared-like. I scrambled out of bed, hurried to the kitchen, got her a glass of water, then hurried back.

"Here," I said. "Can you drink this?"

She nodded and took the glass, sipping slowly, itty-bitty sips, still panting. But she was breathing.

After a moment, many moments, she handed me the glass. "Here," she whispered. "All better. Go on to bed now."

"You sure?" I said.

"I'm sure." She tried to smile, but it was a ghastly kind of smile, her eyes still wide, her lips so white they were almost blue.

I nodded and turned away. I couldn't bear to see

her looking that scared. I went back to the kitchen with the glass and stood feeling my own breath come and go, listening for Monnie's breath. I don't know how long I stood that way, trying to stop being scared, feeling my heart slow down to normal, listening for Monnie.

Finally, I was quieter inside, and I could hear that Monnie was quiet, too, could hear her breathing regular.

"'Night," I called softly, but there was no answer. And I knew she was plumb worn out from the struggle.

I went back to my room, climbed into bed, and snuggled down, making a sort of nest for myself. I listened again to the sounds of the night outside, the wind in the treetops, the movement of the branches. I heard the soft rustle of creatures afoot, and I knew that deer and maybe even coyotes and cougars had made their night trek down the mountain. I closed my eyes then, inviting sleep. I heard the owl, heard it call, but softly this time, softly, softly. And suddenly, I sat up, my heart thudding wildly into my throat. I listened, straining, my heart fluttering. I must have dreamed it.

But no. It came again.

I heard an owl call Monnie's name.

4

For the whole next week, Monnie seemed more weak and frail than ever. There were no more of the coughing fits, but she didn't do hardly any of the things she usually does. She could barely stand up long enough to make a meal. And most nights, she was in bed right after supper. Some mornings, she didn't even get out of bed before I left for school. And she never slept in like that, never before, anyway. But the really scary thing was the garden. She didn't work any more on the garden, not even on the warm days—and we had two or three of them in a row. I knew we had to get in the early peas and radishes and beans. But Monnie didn't do a thing about it. I asked her about it one night when I was sitting at the table doing homework. She was mending an old sweater of mine by the fire, and even from across the room, I could hear her raggedy breathing. But at least this night, she hadn't gone to bed right after supper.

"Don't worry yourself none," she said. "It'll get done. Now get on with your homework. Or next thing you know, I'll be getting a visit from the schoolteacher."

She screwed up her face when she said that, but I just laughed. Monnie's got a distrust of town folks, doesn't like them coming round. Yet she's real tight with the folks up here, knows each one in each house on both sides of the mountain. She knows who married who and when, and which Maren cousin is hooked up with which other Maren cousin, and who is speaking to who and who is not. She even knows the names of each baby born. And that's really saying something, with people like the Cravens having a new baby every year. But town folks, they're not real high on Monnie's list. In fact, if there was school on the mountain, I suspect neither of us would ever go to town. But there is no school up here. So every single day, I trudge about two miles down the valley to the fork where the school bus comes and picks us up, me and the Craven kids and the Zooks, and the Maren boys, back when they were still in school, before they went off to war.

"Miss Ford's not so bad," I said. "She's real young."

"Paints her face," Monnie said. "That's what I heard."

"Maybe a little," I said. Actually, that was one thing I liked about her. She always looked so pretty, so sweet and fresh. "And she smells nice, too," I said. "Jane says she uses toilet water."

"What?" Monnie said.

"No!" I said. "Not like that. Not out of a toilet. It's just called toilet water. It's like—well, like—it's like perfume."

Monnie just shook her head. "Whooeee!" she said. And she said it like she was saying a swear word. Which she doesn't, not ever.

"How you doing in school?" Monnie said.

I looked up at her. "Good," I said.

She nodded.

"Why?" I said. "You know I always do good."

She just shrugged. But there was something on her mind, I could tell. She never asked about my schoolwork, always assumed I was doing good. And I do, maybe because I just love to read. Monnie and me, we don't have many books at home, just the Bible and one book called *Children's Stories* that I have read the cover off. But Miss Ford lends me books— classroom books and sometimes her very own books. Recently she lent me *Little Women,* and I just couldn't put it down. Sometimes I think I'm like the second-oldest sister, Jo, in that book—sort of wild and tempestuous, and wanting to live in exciting places. Other times, I think I'm like Beth, one of Jo's younger sisters, a quiet, stay-at-home person who wants to remain right here on the mountain. Anyway, I do know I'm smart, the smartest one in class except for Ogden Zook. He can add rows and rows of numbers in his head and come up with an answer in two seconds flat.

"Why you asking?" I said again.

Again she just shook her head. But I could tell something was working on her. Well, no sense pushing her. When she was ready to say whatever it was, she'd say it.

I turned back to my book, when suddenly, I heard something—a small squeak, a cry.

I quick looked up at Monnie. But it wasn't her. She had heard it, too, though, and I saw her tilt her head to one side. "A bat," she said.

I looked around, and sure enough, up high on the rafter over the stove, there it was—a tiny, furry creature, not much bigger than my fist.

I sighed and stood up. Bats get in the house sometimes. I kind of like them, actually. They're sweet little furry creatures. But Monnie, she wants nothing to do with them, and when one gets in, she flies around after it like she's a bat herself. Once she spent a whole evening chasing one with a broom, me following with a blanket to throw over it so we could toss it outside into the night. And once, she killed one, squashed it so its little head hung limp to one side and its wings were folded up tight. That made me sad, but I didn't tell her.

"I'll get the blanket," I said. "And the broom."

Monnie just shook her head. "Don't bother," she said.

"Don't bother?" I said.

"Won't kill us," she said.

"But . . ."

"But nothing. Let it be," she said.

I just stared at her. Monnie's afraid of bats. Monnie hates bats. She despises bats.

She was too sick to chase a bat.

"I can do it myself," I said quietly. And I started for the porch where we keep the broom.

"No need to get all het up about it," she said again. "We don't bother him, he won't bother us."

I came back to the table slowly. I sat down and looked at Monnie. She looked right back at me.

"Maybe I'll go in to the clinic tomorrow," she said.

I just stared at her. The clinic? In town? Monnie go to town? Monnie go to a doctor? She never goes to a doctor. Yes, she takes me to the clinic once in a while, like when I used to get croup a lot. And I had my vaccinations when I was little. But for herself? Monnie just goes to Ellie for herbs when she's sick, like when she gets a rash from poison ivy or a queasy stomach or needs to get her blood thickened up for winter. I could feel my heart thumping hard, but I tried to keep my face still and calm. "Okay," I said. "That's good, I think."

"You can go with me. You can miss a day's school, right?"

"Sure," I said.

"You're doing good," she said.

So that's what those questions had been all about. "Yes," I said. "I'm doing good."

"Think you could drive?" she said.

"What?" I said. "Drive? Me drive?"

"Why not?" she said. "It's not all that hard. Just point the car on the road and keep your foot ready to brake. I'll show you before we start out." She put aside her mending and started to hoist herself to her feet. I could hear her labored breathing, rough, harsh in her chest.

I wanted to hurry across and help her. But I knew I couldn't. She wouldn't want help. But she did want me to drive her to the clinic. And what did I know about driving? Nothing.

"I'm going on to bed," she said. "I'll close my door so that there creature won't get in." She nodded up at the rafter. "Close yours, too."

I nodded. "Okay," I said.

Monnie frowned at me. "And stop looking scared, like you seen a ghost in the mirror. It's just a bat. And it's just driving a car."

I laughed, couldn't help it. My heart shows on my face. Monnie tells me that all the time.

But she was wrong. It wasn't the bat I was scared about. And it wasn't driving a car.

Those were not the things that troubled me at all.

5

We don't use the car often, mostly because Monnie hardly ever goes to town. And now, with the war on, and shortages of everything, sugar and chocolate—even gas—well, the car just sits there, except for once in a while like now.

Before we left that morning, Monnie told me to put a pillow on the seat to raise me up, and we moved the seat forward so I could reach the pedals. Then she showed me how to make the car go. It was kind of easy coming down the mountain. I did just like Monnie said—put one foot on the gas, other on the brake, and let the car find its own way. It more or less did, too, as if it felt the road beneath the wheels. All I had to do was guide the steering wheel a bit, and brake when it got to going too fast. But then we got to town. I didn't know about blinking lights, and suddenly, there were horns honking and cars going here and there and turning in front of me. Lord, I was real scared. But we got to the clinic and parked. I'd done it. And Monnie was so pleased.

"See?" she said. "I knew you could do it. From now on, driving's your job."

I just leaned my head back against the car seat. My heart was beating so fast, I wasn't sure I wanted that job again. "Unless I get caught," I said.

She made a face. "Who's going to catch you?" she said. And she began hoisting herself out of the car.

I hurried around to help her. All the way in the car, she'd been wheezing bad, stopping to suck in her breath, then wheezing some more. I didn't see how she could even manage to stand up, as little breath as she had.

But when I went to help her, she just shook off my arm. "Let me be," she said. "I got this far, can get inside all right." She squinted at me. "You want to wait out here?"

I shook my head. "It's okay," I said. "I'll go in."

I knew why she asked. Neither of us can abide the clinic. It's not the doctors. There's two of them, a dentist and a doctor. They're mostly pretty nice, especially Dr. Harkins, who's been here as long as anyone can remember. Even though he's a town doctor, he knows about mountain people. He's not all bossy and obnoxious, thinking he knows better than everybody. Once he came all the way up mountain to see Hector Maren when he got snakebite. And when Dr. Harkins got there, he just looked Hector over, and he said Ellie had treated Hector just right, he couldn't have done better himself. Sure enough, in a day or two, Hector was as good as new. And Dr. Harkins didn't charge nothing for his visit, either. Monnie trusts him. It's why she let him care for me when I got croup so bad, when even Ellie's herbs and steam tents didn't work. But it's the others, the social worker and the nurse, that neither of us can abide. The social worker's name is Miss Cotter, and she's new here—just about five years she's been around—and all the mountain people hate her. I think town people hate her, too, but I'm not sure. She has a long face, long nose, and beady little eyes, so she looks like a wolf. She's sharp as a wolf, too, and just as sneaky. She gets into your business and asks the most personal things, like how are you getting along in school, and do you have any friends. When I come here, I pretend not to hear what she says. Once she even had Dr. Harkins check my hearing. Which was just fine, and after he checked my ears, he winked at me. I think he knew what was what.

The nurse, Miss Dorris, she's the same nurse who comes to school. And though she doesn't ask questions straight out like Miss Cotter does, you can tell she's nosing around and will report back to Miss Cotter on everything she sees. Like once, she came to school to weigh and measure all of us, and when it was my turn, she clucked and clucked over how much I weighed—actually how little I weighed. Next thing you know, I got called into her office, and Miss Cotter's there, too. And they wanted to know, was I getting enough to eat, and did Monnie and me have enough money? And they'd like to check what I had brought for lunch that day.

Well.

I opened my lunch bag and showed them my peanut butter sandwich and my whole cabbage cut up into quarter sections and the orange. And then I told them I have a perfectly average weight for my build, and I am small built because my mama was small built, and I know that for a fact. And I told them they had no business pushing their pointy noses into other people's business. If they wanted to ask such personal questions, I said, I might want to have a lawyer with me next time. Now, I don't know where I got that from, but it just popped into my head. And then Miss Cotter said, Well, we'll see about that, maybe we'll have a lawyer ourselves, and she and Miss Dorris looked at each other, and I could tell they were laughing at me. But I notice neither of them has bothered me again in a long time.

When I told Monnie about it, she just howled with laughter.

Anyway, that's why Monnie asked if I was going into the clinic. I was. I wouldn't let her face this on her own. So up the steps we went, and it was hard going for Monnie. And finally, we got ourselves settled in the waiting room and sat down to wait our turn. Miss Dorris nodded at us when we came in, but she never even said, How do.

So I called her a name. But just inside my head.

There was only one person ahead of us, a skinny mama with two babies with runny noses, and all of them, the mama, too, coughing harsh coughs that sounded like they were barking. I picked up a magazine and handed one to Monnie, but she just waved me off. She sat straight up in her chair, clasping and unclasping her hands, her swollen feet scraping back and forth in her slipper shoes, all fidgety-like. It's not just the clinic that does that to Monnie. It's being in town. She says she can't see why a body could ever live in town, when the mountain is there. But then, like Monnie says, with some folks, there's no figuring.

We weren't there more'n about five minutes when Miss Dorris called the mama and babies inside, and then, right after, Monnie. Monnie stood up as straight as I've seen her in a while. But she was breathing so hard and wheezy, I could hear her from across the room. I watched her go, and I noticed that partway down the hall, Miss Dorris took her arm. And Monnie didn't shake her off.

I picked up the magazine again. It was *Life*, and I got all caught up by the pictures of children, wide eyed and scared-looking, one of them a girl about my age. They had been bombed out of their homes in England, and they looked at me so sad-like, their eyes as big as owl eyes. Under the pictures was a story asking for homes for them here.

The mountain would be a safe place for them. I wondered if I should ask Monnie if we could take an orphan to live with us, maybe that girl my age who was in the pictures. She was pretty and she looked sweet, and I thought about how she and I could talk about things, girl talk, like Monnie says. I've always wanted a sister. I was even dividing up my room, one side for Alice—that's the name I gave her—and one side for me. And then . . . well, then I thought about Monnie and how sick she was. And I thought maybe it wouldn't be such a good idea to bring Alice home with us, even if she did live in London and had to duck bombs at night. At least in London, she had her mother and father with her. I guess she did.

I sat up and looked at the wall clock, watched it

tick off the seconds, watched the hand jump ahead, one minute, two minutes, twenty minutes, half an hour. I hoped that the doctor was doing something good to Monnie, maybe giving her medicine to help her breathing.

Across the room, behind a little glass half wall, Miss Dorris was standing with Miss Cotter, the two of them buzz-buzzing away. They kept cutting their eyes at me, and I knew they were talking about me.

Well, let them.

I started thinking about my best friend, Jane, and what had happened to her and her brothers. Jane's papa drinks some, especially on Friday nights and Saturdays. Well, other days, too. And when he drinks he gets mean, and Jane and her brothers hide out till he quiets down. Sometimes they just go outside, or else, if it's dark, they hide in the old root cellar by the apple orchard. That way, nobody gets hurt, and nobody's the worse for wear, because by morning, he's usually fine. But Miss Cotter, she heard about it somehow, and next thing you know, the whole family's broken up. Jane's living in a big fancy house in town with the preacher and his wife—not Reverend Tucker, but the town preacher, Reverend Hornby, who is a dreadful, mean man. She brings sandwiches to school that are made from store-bought white bread, cut up into little triangles, and she's scrubbed so clean her face shines pink, and she has nice new clothes. But her little brothers are living with some folks on the other side of the hollow and she hasn't seen them in months and hasn't seen her daddy, either. At recess in the back lot, Jane cries by herself sometimes.

I sighed and looked at the clock again. Almost an hour now.

I looked over at the little glassed-in room. Miss Dorris had gone, but Miss Cotter was sitting at the desk, and she caught my eye. "Blessing?" she said. "Come on back here and talk to me."

She smiled then. At least, the corners of her mouth moved up, but her eyes stayed flat and mean. She wiggled her fingers, beckoning me to her.

Well, why should I? I could say no, real polite-like. But then I got up and went over, because she might have something to tell me about Monnie.

"Come in," she said. "Sit down."

I came in. But I stayed standing. "It's all right, ma'am."

"Sit," she said. "Be comfortable."

"I'm comfortable, ma'am," I said.

"Suit yourself," she said. "So, how are you, Blessing? I haven't seen you in a while."

I nodded. "I'm fine, thank you, ma'am."

"Staying well? No more croup attacks?"

"No, ma'am."

"You've grown a little, seems to me," she said, squinching up her eyes at me.

I didn't answer that. But inside my head, I said, *You, too.* 'Cause she had. She'd gotten fat.

"And how's school?"

"Fine, ma'am," I said.

She looked down at her desk. There was silence then. I wanted to ask about Monnie, but I thought it best to just wait. I've learned with grown folk— sometimes they just got to do things their own way.

Her evil little eyes were darting this way and that, from me to this notebook on the desk in front of her, and I remembered how I always thought of her as a wolf. A wolf in a pack of sheep, picking out the one that best suited her fancy.

"So you're making out all right?" she asked, finally. "You and your grandma?"

"Yes, ma'am," I said.

"Good, good!" she said. She leaned forward over the desk, folding her hands together. "I do wish you'd sit down." She laughed, but it didn't sound like she was happy, and her eyes didn't smile.

"I'm really fine here, ma'am."

She sighed. "So, your grandma does all right? Cooks and keeps house and takes care of you?" she asked.

"Yes, ma'am," I said.

"But you're not in school today," she said.

"No, ma'am."

"Your grandma needed your help today?"

"No, ma'am," I said. I knew I needed to think quick. "I didn't feel good last night," I said. "I . . . had a sore throat. Just a little one. But Monnie didn't think I should be around other kids today. And she didn't want me to stay home alone."

I could see what was coming. And I wasn't giving her any excuse to get her claws into me like she had with Jane.

"Well, you don't look too sick," she said. "You had breakfast?"

"Yes, ma'am," I said. Then suddenly, something evil took over me, and words just popped out of my mouth, words I didn't even know I was going to say. "Monnie cooked up a whole bear last night," I said.

"Oh," she said. And then she suddenly looked up at me. "A bear?" she said, as if it had just sunk in. "She cooked a whole bear? Where'd she get bear?"

"Why, she caught it, ma'am," I said. "Trapped it herself, then skinned it, everything."

Which of course was a big fat lie. But there it was. Let her figure it out.

"Well," she said.

I knew she didn't believe me, but what could she

do about it? She sure couldn't prove I was lying.

"How did you get here today?" she asked.

"In the car, ma'am," I said. And because I was afraid of what was coming, I quick added, "We had enough stamps left on our ration card." Which was not what she was going to ask about, I knew. She was going to ask if Monnie was strong enough to drive. "We haven't used the car but once this winter."

And now my heart was really racing.

"I see," she said.

"Where's Monnie?" I said. "It's taking a while."

And then I heard voices—Monnie's voice, and she sounded good, strong, and I heard her laugh.

I stepped out into the hallway, and there was Monnie walking toward me. Dr. Harkins was with her, holding her arm, and the two of them looked pleasant enough, not worried, just kind of smiling and chatty-like. I felt my heart soar.

When Monnie saw me there, she turned herself loose from Dr. H. "There's Blessing," she said. "I'll be going now."

"Take care of yourself," he said. And then he waved to me and went back down the hall.

"You okay?" I said, and I took her arm. And this time she let me.

"Will be when I'm out of here," she said softly.

The two of us got ourselves into the car, and I didn't care who saw me driving, didn't care if I was scared silly of driving, we got ourselves out and away. Never in my whole life had I been so glad to be back on Star Mountain.

6

Later that night I was by the fire, reading *Little Women*, and Monnie was across from me, playing gently on her fiddle. I had felt fidgety ever since we got back home, wondering when Monnie was going to tell me more about the clinic visit. But all she had said was, "I'm sick and I'm old, and I ain't getting better." She said it straight out, even laughing a little, like it was no big thing. But there was pain in her voice, and I heard it.

Still, she *was* better, some anyway. I figured the medicine she got was helping. She was playing "Dear Companion," one of her favorites, when I looked up and saw she was watching me.

"Don't you let that social worker wolf get her claws into you," she said when she saw me look up. "You hear?"

"We won't," I said. "We're smarter than her by a lot."

"Not talking *we*," she said. "I'm talking 'bout you."

I blinked at her, my heart beginning a little thumping dance.

"Reckon you can manage that?" she said.

"Me?" I said.

She nodded.

I just looked at her. "What are you talking about?" I said.

"You know. That Cotter woman," Monnie said. "She ain't no better than a wolf, not even good as a wolf. A wolf, he kills to eat, don't kill for no reason. But you're smart. You'll outsmart her good."

I looked away, felt my heart thumping crazily in my throat.

"Told you I ain't getting out of this one alive," she said. "So we got to find our way round that Cotter wolf."

"You brought home medicine," I said.

"That I did," she said.

"To make you better," I said. "To make you *better*."

"Not better, girl," Monnie said softly. "Ain't getting better and I already told you that. Doctor said so. And not just that—I pretty much knowed it before I went. He just agreed, that's all. So that's that."

"You don't know that!" I said. "*He* doesn't know!"

"I know what I know," Monnie said, still softly.

"You can't know, so don't talk like a fool!" I said. I glared at her, then picked up my book and opened it again.

Don't think about Monnie, I told myself. *Think about Beth—quiet, sweet soul—and rambunctious Jo. Think about them.* And I did, I concentrated on them. Poor Beth was sick again. She's so quiet, so uncomplaining, and her big sister is so wild, tumultuous.

But the thoughts crept back in. Monnie wasn't getting better. I never should have let her go to the clinic just to hear bad stuff. Besides, what do doctors know? Monnie always says that. So why was she listening to him this time?

Because she already knew. Knew from inside her.

No.

Yes.

I heard the owl call her name.

I kept reading, trying to read. But I couldn't get inside that book, no matter how wonderful Beth was. I could just feel Monnie looking at me, watching me, studying me.

Finally I shut my book and looked up at her.

"What?" I said, impatient-like.

"You were given to me to care for," Monnie said, "and I aim to keep caring for you. And part of that is . . ."

"Foolishness," I said. "It's all fool talk, that's all it is. You talk like an outright fool. What's got into you? You never talked this way before!"

Monnie laughed then, surprising me, a loud, yelping wheezy kind of sound. After a minute, when she had caught her breath, she said, "Well, well. Who knows? Maybe it is fool talk, and maybe it ain't."

"Is!" I said.

She laughed even harder, her breath coming in little wheezy spurts. When she had quieted down, she said, "Girl? Maybe you're right. Maybe we ain't got no cause to start talking like this yet. We can let it go awhile. There's time enough."

"Time for more fool talk?" I said. Then, because I was feeling hurtful and hateful, I added, "And 'ain't' is not a word!"

Monnie gave me one of her la-di-da looks.

"And you can't say, 'Ain't got no,'" I went on, feeling the hurt welling up inside me, mean and hateful. "'Ain't got no' is a double negative, Miss Ford said so. It's the same thing as saying you do have some. So there."

"And that," Monnie said, yelping laughter again,

"ain't what you meant at all!"

I glared at her.

She lifted one hand, like she was patting the air space between us—or patting me. "Don't fret," she said quietly. "We'll manage. We always do. We got a little time yet to figure it out."

I didn't even bother to glare at her. I just got up and went to my room, shutting the door tight behind me. Shutting me in. Shutting her out. If she was dead set on talking about stuff like that, I was dead set on not listening to her. And I can be every bit as stubborn as she can, more so if I want.

But I swear, Monnie was a wizard or a witch, because when I went to sleep, she was there again, right in my dream. I didn't even invite her, but there she was. In my dream, I am all grown-up and have a baby of my own. I'm holding that baby, sitting in the rocking chair where I sat tonight, across the room from Monnie, and she's stroking that fiddle, playing "What'll I Do with the Baby-o, If He Won't Go to Sleepy-o." And I look up and Monnie is smiling at me, like she's been looking at me a long time. I smile back at her, and then I get up, and I'm crossing the room, and I put that baby in her arms, right up close to her heart. I can feel her heart beating, nice and strong, nice and strong, and I smile at her and she smiles back. Next thing you know, there's a procession starting. Monnie is leading it, carrying that baby, and all the mountain people are following her, walking away from me. And then they all disappear down a long corridor. I turn back and look at my house. I watch then as all the lamps in the house go out, one by one, till there's just the one shining in Monnie's room. And then that goes out, too.

I woke from the dream, my face wet. I lay on my back, staring up at the ceiling, feeling the tears run back into my ears. I know what the dream meant. She came into my dream, came to tell me something. She's telling me the very same thing she was trying to tell me before, that she's getting ready to leave me. And she's taking my baby child with her—that part of me that loves her.

That part that won't be able to go on without her.

For a long time I lay awake. Outside my window the stars were so thick, so close, I almost felt I could reach out and touch them, feel them cold and hard like diamonds. And I thought. And thought. Monnie had brought home some medicine. What was medicine for, but to make you better?

But Monnie had said no, not better. Just a little something to help the cough.

So maybe she was right. Maybe she wasn't going to get better. But maybe, too, she wasn't going to get worse. You could just stay sick for a long while, couldn't you? Look at Reverend Tucker's wife. She had been sick for ages. And she was still alive.

I got up then, went to the window, and looked out. In the room next to mine, Monnie's light was on. I could see the square of light outside on the grass. And I could hear her breathing. Even through the walls, I could hear her struggle for each breath. I wanted to go in to her, to say, It's all right. If you have to talk about this, you can. But how could I let her talk about going away, about . . . dying? Yes, that was the word. I'd said it right out in my head.

And there was something more, something selfish: What would happen to me? Who would I live with? There was no one. There was just Monnie, and just me, ever since I was little. And I was only eleven years old. I couldn't live alone. Or could I? That's why Monnie was talking about social worker wolves. She was thinking about what would happen to me.

But Monnie got married when she was just fifteen years old. She's told me that a million times. That wasn't that many more years off for me. Not that I'd get married. But if Monnie could be grown up at fifteen, why couldn't I be grown up at eleven? Or maybe I'd be twelve, or even thirteen. Monnie could live a long time yet, a long, long time.

I don't know how long I stood there, looking out at the stars, listening to the branch scratching the windowpane, the wind rushing in the treetops. The owl was hooting to his mate off in the woods, and she was hooting back, and they both sounded lonesome, like they were sorrowing over a loss, or maybe over the distance between them.

Outside on the grass, I saw Monnie's light wink off. I went back to bed and pulled the covers tight around my ears, shutting out the sounds of the owls calling, the sound of the wind. Shutting out my thoughts.

7

Next morning, I was about dead. I was so sleepy in class, I could hardly keep my eyes from drooping closed. Jane had been looking at me all morning, signaling me with her eyes, so I knew she had something to tell me. And I was itching to talk to her, too, to tell her about Monnie and about me driving to town.

At recess, Jane grabbed me and pulled me over to the side of the schoolyard. "Guess what happened last night?" she said, before I could even say a word. "Reverend Hornby got mad at Mrs. Hornby. He didn't like his dinner because he said it was cold. So know what he did?"

I shook my head.

"He dumped it in the dog's dish!" she said. "Got right up from the table and dumped it in the dish.

And then he told Mrs. Hornby to make him a new dinner."

"Did not!" I said.

"Did too!" Jane said.

"Did she do it?" I said.

"Yup."

"I don't believe you! She made him another dinner?"

Jane nodded. "Yup. She did."

"Wow!" I said. "I'd have told him to make himself his own dinner and lick it out of the dog's dish, thank you very much."

She shook her head. "Nobody talks back to him."

"I would," I said.

Jane shrugged. "Yeah," she said. "But you're brave."

"So? You're brave," I said.

"Ha!" Jane said. "And then, know what he did after he got his supper? I was trying real hard not to laugh, and he saw me. And he said, You think this is funny, don't you? And I said, Well no, not funny, and he said Yes you do, and you're not only irreverent, you're a liar. So he made us kneel down after supper, right there at the table. And he prayed over me for being a sinner."

"I hate him," I said.

"Me, too. When he makes us pray, I just pray to

53

go home." She sighed. "My pa's not so bad."

"I know," I said.

"So he gets drunk sometimes," she said.

I just nodded.

"When he's wild in his head, we hide in the cellar. Or in closets. He can't get at us there. And in the morning, he's fine again."

"I know," I said.

She sighed again. "I miss Johnny and Buck so bad. Even though they're a pain sometimes, I miss them bad. And I worry about Buck and his being sick and if he gets his medicine all right."

I nodded and sighed. But what could I say? Even I missed them, especially little Buck, with his eyes as big as quarters. He has something wrong with him, I don't know what it's called, but he gets seizures and he just shakes all over and his eyes roll up in his head. Jane takes real good care of him. Just thinking about them made me feel sad, and I'm not even their sister. I mean, I'd want to stay with my brothers and even my drunken daddy. At least, they'd all be my own. And we'd be together.

"So how come you weren't in school yesterday?" Jane asked. "You sick?"

"No. Monnie was. We went to the clinic."

"She sick again?" Jane said.

"Still sick," I said.

"What did they do for her? She get medicine?"

"Yeah, but it won't make her better."

"Well, that's dumb. Then why give it to her?"

I just shrugged. "For her cough," I said. "But you know what I thought of this morning? Know how Ellie knows about herbs and all?"

Jane nodded.

"I'm going to ask her what she can think of to help Monnie."

"Monnie's probably already asked her, right?"

I looked away. I hadn't thought of that. Of course Monnie would have asked Ellie already. And maybe Monnie had already tried herbs and not even told me, tea and things that I wouldn't even have noticed.

I sighed, suddenly remembering something I used to do when I was little—I used to make up lists, lists of things I would do when I grew up. My favorite list was all the things I would buy for Monnie when I made a whole lot of money someday.

"What?" Jane asked now, as if she were listening into my thoughts.

I just shook my head. "Guess what?" I said. "I drove to the clinic."

"You're lying!"

"Am not."

"You don't know how to drive."

"I do now."

"Wow!" Jane breathed. "Is it hard? Why did you drive?"

"I told you. Monnie was too sick."

"Oh," Jane said. She pulled at my sleeve. "Come on. Let's go sit."

There's a huge cottonwood tree in the center of the schoolyard, and nobody was under it right then. We sat down, leaning our backs against it. It was cold, but there was a thin sunlight peeping through the clouds, and it felt good to sit and soak up the sun.

We each picked up little twigs and began drawing squiggles in the dirt.

"Monnie'll get better," Jane said after a bit. "I know she will. She's not that sick. Why don't you go back to the clinic? Ask Dr. Harkins yourself?"

"Why?" I said.

"Why not?" Jane said. "Maybe he told Monnie something and she's not telling you."

"Like what?"

"I don't know," Jane answered. "But you know how people are, especially old folks like Monnie. Maybe she just doesn't want to have an operation or something. Not that I blame her."

I knew why she said that. Her pa always says that the hospital killed her mama. But it didn't. Her pa killed her, I figure, made her mama so sad that she just upped and died to get away from him.

"No," I said now. "Monnie would've told me. Besides, the hospital's in town. Monnie would never leave the mountain."

"Maybe you could talk her into it or something."

Actually, Monnie *had* said something about how Dr. Harkins wanted her to have oxygen. She said she told him she'd rather breathe on her own or not at all. Maybe oxygen would help. Maybe . . .

"You come with me," I said.

She shook her head, tugging at the hair around her temple where Mrs. Hornby pulls it tight back into a ponytail. "Can't," she said. "Every day, he makes us do something. Today it's Bible study. Tomorrow, study hymns. I miss one of his church things, he *kills* me."

Miss Ford came out then and began ringing the bell, a big old metal thing with a handle. Everybody scurries into line as soon as she starts, but she just smiles and keeps right on going. She must get a kick out of the noise.

Jane and I waited till the line formed, then got in at the end, behind Edith and her sidekick, Dorothy. They're town girls, and so snotty you can't believe it. Edith has fine, store-bought clothes from Sears. And Dorothy's papa owns the dry goods store, so she always has new things to wear, and new pencils and a pencil case. The two of them are always together and they pretend they're better than everyone else, especially better than Jane and me. Well, especially better than Jane. I think everybody still remembers Jane's flour-sack coat and her brown teeth.

Now they both moved a little away from us, like we had bugs or something.

Most days, it doesn't bother me if they snub me something awful. But I was feeling mean about things, and kind of sorry for Jane. So I gave Dorothy a flat tire—stepped on the back of her shoe, so it came off her heel. When she turned and glared at me, I gave her a big, fake smile.

"Sorry," I whispered. I held out my arm, so she could hold on to me while she tried to wriggle back into her shoe.

"I'm telling!" she said. She turned back and took Edith's arm instead.

The line started to move then and we all filed back into school. Miss Ford always reads to us after recess, and today she was going to finish *David Copperfield*. I just love that story, love Charles Dickens. I think he really knows what it's like to be a kid. But even after she started reading, and the words of the story were flowing into my head, my mind kept drifting back to the clinic. Maybe I should go there after school. I wasn't going to do what Monnie was doing—just give up on getting better. I was going to do something.

I would go to the clinic. Though even thinking about it gave me shudders.

8

When school let out, Jane and I walked to the end of town together the way we always do before we go our separate ways—me up mountain, her off to the preacher's house. Used to be, we walked all the way up home together, if we had decided against the school bus. This day, she didn't poke questions at me about going to the clinic, and I was grateful for that. Jane knows just when to shut up.

Inside my head, I was still fussing about whether to go. I mean, it's scary, especially since Miss Cotter would be there. But I had to try. Maybe there was something Monnie could do, like oxygen. If I knew for sure, I could talk her into it.

When we got to the edge of town, Jane looked at me, her eyebrows up.

"I'm going," I said. "But I'm scared."

She laughed. "Trade places? You go to the preacher's for me?"

I shuddered. "No, thanks," I said.

"My fingers are crossed," she said, holding them up so I could see.

"Thanks," I said.

I stood for a minute and watched her head off to the preacher's house, thinking how she looks a whole lot better on the outside than she used to, her clothes clean and new, her teeth brushed. But it's what's on the inside that counts. What she had said about her pa and her brothers had made me so sad. I guess I was thinking about myself, too—how it would be for me if Monnie died. Which I would not think about. So I turned and took myself down the street to the clinic.

I climbed those steps and walked inside, my head up, my heart thundering away like crazy. I glanced around the waiting room—no one there. But in the little cubicle behind the glass window was Miss Cotter. I went up to her, my mouth dry and cottony feeling. "I want to see Dr. Harkins, please," I said.

"You were just here yesterday," she said. "You sick?"

I shook my head. "No," I said. "I just want to talk to him about Monnie."

"What about her?" Miss Cotter said, her eyebrows raised.

"Just *about* her, is all."

Miss Cotter frowned at me. Her eyebrows were drawn on in pencil, and even though she was frowning, her fake eyebrows made her look surprised. It was like one part of her face didn't know what the other part was doing. "Did your grandma send you?" she asked.

"No. I sent me."

"And what do you want?"

"I just want to *talk* to him," I said. "I need to talk about my grandma."

Miss Cotter shook her head. "I'm afraid not," she said.

"Not? Why? Isn't he here?"

Miss Cotter shook her head again. She was wearing a plain black dress, and her hair flowed down around her shoulders and she had to keep tilting her head this way and that to keep it out of her face. Her hair is gray, and with that black dress and her sharp nose, she looked just like a witch. "He's here. But that's privileged information," she said. "Doctor won't tell anyone else about his patient's business."

"But she's my grandma!"

"I'm sorry," she said.

Well, she wasn't sorry. And I hadn't come here to be told no. So I said again, very loud, "I need to see Dr. Harkins. I need him now."

She just shrugged and shook her head again.

"Look," I said, and I tried to sound reasonable, grown-up. "See, she's mine and I'm hers, we're all the other has, so he can tell me whatever he told her."

I thought that would make her feel better, more secure-like. But no. Some people, they're so bound and determined to have their own way, a grizzly bear couldn't budge them.

"I'm sorry, Blessing," she said. And then, just like that, she slid closed the little glass window. Leaving her inside. Me outside.

I didn't wait even one little second. I scurried past her cubicle, down the little hallway, past the examining rooms, peeking into each room as I went. In about half a second, I heard her heels clicking on the linoleum right after me.

"Here! Stop!" she called. "You can't do this."

Oh, no? Well, I can, and I am. And I kept on going, faster, till I was at the end of the hall, peeking into each room along the way. But nobody was in the rooms, no doctor, no patient, not even Miss Dorris, nobody at all. Until I got to the end of the hall, and there was Dr. Harkins's office. He was sitting there with Dr. Moss, the dentist, and both of them looked up in surprise.

"What's up?" Dr. Harkins said. "Hey, Blessing. Need something?"

Miss Cotter had caught up with me, and she reached for me, but I ducked away from her hand.

"I need to talk to you," I said to Dr. Harkins.

"I'm sorry, Doctors," Miss Cotter said, breathing hard. "She just pushed right past me! Right past me."

"I did not!" I said, whirling around to face her. "You closed your window on me."

"Whoa!" Dr. Moss said.

Both doctors were standing by then, and Dr. Harkins came to the doorway. "Why don't you come in here, Blessing, and talk to me," he said. He nodded at Dr. Moss. "Talk to you later, Sam," he said. And then to Miss Cotter, he said, "It's okay now. And thank you for bringing her back here."

"Well!" she said. "I didn't bring her back. And it's very impertinent of her to come barging in this way."

"Let me take care of it, all right?" Dr. Harkins said.

He closed the door and motioned me to a seat.

He sat down behind his desk and grinned. "Whew!" he said.

"She chased me!" I said.

He just smiled. "She was trying to do her job. So what's up? How's things with you? It's been a while since I saw you. I mean, a while since I talked to you."

"'Cause I haven't been sick," I said.

"That's good," he said. And he smiled at me, his blue eyes crinkling up around the corners. I wondered how old he was—as old as Monnie?

He didn't say anything more, and I fiddled around with a pencil from his desk. I like Dr. Harkins, but I felt a little nervous. What if Miss Cotter was right? What if he wouldn't tell me anything? What if he said like she did, that it was privileged information?

I swallowed hard. "I want to ask you about Monnie," I said, looking up at him.

He nodded and kept right on looking at me. "What about her?" he said.

"You know," I said. "I want to know how she is. And . . . everything. But I'm scared that . . . well, Miss Cotter said you wouldn't tell me because it's privileged patient-doctor talk."

"Oh," he said, "don't worry about that."

"Really?"

"Really. Don't tell her I told you, though. So you want to know about your grandma."

I nodded.

He was quiet then, and I didn't say anything, either, just waited. He picked up a pipe from his desk and began fiddling with it, stuffing it full of tobacco, and then lighting it up. All this took a whole lot of time, but I didn't get mad. I could see from his face he was working on something.

After a minute, he looked up at me. "Let me get her chart. You sit there."

Where else would I go? And then he went away, taking his pipe with him. Which was a shame, since I'd been thinking that it might have been nice to try a puff or two.

When he was gone, I took a deep breath, feeling a little more cheerful. If he had to look things up in her chart, maybe it wasn't as bad as Monnie had said. He'd remember if he was going to tell me she was dying, right?

Even though I've been to the clinic a bunch of times, I'd never been in Dr. Harkins's office before. There were all sorts of framed things on the walls— something-something medical school, something of the Appalachians, Tennessee school of something, all of them saying he had graduated and was smart, I guess. But why put those boring things up there? I mean, he already knows he's been to school, so he doesn't need to prove it to himself. And his patients already know it, or we wouldn't be here. If it were my office, I'd put up a nice scene of the valley in spring, or deer in the meadow on the side of the mountain. Maybe even a picture of Jesus with children.

I got up and checked out the papers on his desk.

There was nothing interesting there though, just letters and notes and squiggly doodles.

A few minutes later he was back, carrying a folder. "Tell you what," he said, sitting down at his desk. "I'll make you a deal. You come visit me every so often and talk to me." He lowered his voice. "And I'll tell you what I can about what's in this file and about your grandma."

I could tell from the way he was acting that he was letting me know he was breaking the rules doing this. His voice got real low, and he acted very sneaky-like, looking over his shoulder at the doorway like he thought Miss Cotter would peep in and tell on him.

I thought, I can play this game, too, and I said, "Okay. I'll come talk to you." Because I was thinking, Well, what do I know? Maybe he's lonely. I know for a fact he has no children, and his wife died long ago. Besides, if I can get some information, it's worth it.

He put the file down, but he didn't even open it up, just folded his hands on top of it and looked straight at me.

"What did your grandma tell you?" he said.

I looked straight back at him. "She told me how sick she was," I said. "She even said she wasn't going to get better."

"I'll tell you what I told her," he said slowly. And

by the look on his face, I knew it was nothing but bad news coming, and I felt my heart thumping madly again.

"She's an old, old woman, you know," he said.

"Not that old," I said.

"Old enough," he said. "And all those years haven't been kind to her."

I nodded.

"Well," he said. "She's very sick. I'm afraid she's very, very sick."

"I know that," I said. "She told me that yesterday." And then I decided to level with him, because after all, that's what I was here for. "But see, what I wonder is—is there anything we can do to make her better? I mean, I know Monnie. She's stubborn. Maybe she should be in the hospital or something? Or be on oxygen?"

Now that I was actually saying it, it sounded dumb. Why did I think he could tell me something to help Monnie when he hadn't told her anything? But still, I couldn't help hoping.

"You're right," he said. "We could try some hospital rest. We could try oxygen. But what would you say if I said—it won't matter? None of it will really make a difference?"

I waited, my heart thundering away.

"You see," he said, "none of it will help. Not really. It won't change the outcome."

"Outcome?"

"I mean . . ." He closed his mouth, opened it again, closed it.

Suddenly I was mad at him, real, real mad at him. *Mealymouthed,* I thought. *Chicken freak. Scared cat.* So after a minute, I said it straight out. "You mean, the outcome is—no matter what, she's going to die? Right?"

I said the word *die,* right hard and loud.

"I'm sorry, Blessing," he said, soft-like. "I'm real, real sorry."

I got up then. No sense wasting time. If she wasn't getting better, she wasn't getting better. But somewhere in my heart, I didn't believe him, either. You just do not give up on somebody so easy-like. Not when that person is Monnie.

And yet, maybe I did believe him, or sort of believe him. Because my heart felt fit to bust.

The minute I stood up, he stood up, too. "Don't go," he said. "We can still talk."

I shook my head.

"Why not?" he said.

I just looked at him.

All I feel like talking about is ways to make Monnie

69

better. And you said she's not going to get better. So what's left to talk about? But I didn't say that out loud.

I looked away then because suddenly tears came welling up in my eyes. I don't know what I had been hoping for. I'd known before I even went that there was nothing to be done. Monnie had said so. And Monnie doesn't lie to me, not ever.

I just shook my head. Last night, I had told Monnie she was being a fool, talking fool talk. But she wasn't the fool. I was.

"Blessing?" Dr. Harkins said. "You said you'd come and talk to me. Will you?"

I shook my head no.

"You said you would," he said again.

I shrugged.

"Next Wednesday?" he said. "Same time?"

I sucked in my breath and looked at him. "But— you said Monnie won't get better," I said. "Right?"

He sighed. "Blessing, I did say that," he said. "But I could be wrong. Nobody can ever say that for sure. She might. Miracles have happened before."

"But it would take a miracle?" I said.

"Sometimes the body performs its own miracles. I've seen some pretty amazing things in my time."

Yes. And right then, I made up my mind—*again.* I was not giving up. He was going to see amazing things again. I didn't know how I'd manage it. But I wasn't going to give up, just because he was giving up. Maybe Ellie could help. Or else something. But maybe next week, I'd come back and tell him something amazing. I wasn't giving up.

9

I was late getting home that day, but I knew Monnie wouldn't be worried. Many days I stayed out awhile with Jane—at least, I did before she went to the preacher's house. Other times, I just wander on the mountain, singing, or picking flowers, or following the trail of a fox or a coyote. Sometimes I stop and visit a neighbor.

But this day, I had stayed so long at the clinic that it was blue-black by the time I got home, the dark already settled over the mountain. Stars were out, peeping through the blanket of night sky, scattering themselves every which way, a few here, a few there. There was no pattern I could see, no Big Dipper, no Little Dipper, no Orion, nothing familiar. It was just a mess of stars, like ice chips thrown across the sky.

The tree branches whipped back and forth above

me, and the wind made its little lonesome sound, crying softly through the trees. Off in the meadow, a lark called good night and was answered by a sudden chorus of tree frogs, shouting out their mating songs.

In front of me, our cabin lay full in the moonlight, the roof reflecting starlight. Not a single lamp shone from within.

I began to hurry then, realizing just how late I was, hoping Monnie was all right. I opened the cabin door, and the moonlight rushed in before me, lighting my way.

I quick lit a lamp, made my way to Monnie's room.

No Monnie. Her bed was empty.

I had a sudden awful thought. She had tried to work outside in the garden, and she'd tumbled right off the edge of the ravine where a fox or a mountain lion would find her and . . .

Fool thought!

I spun around and hurried back to the big room. And there, sitting by the window in the light of the moon and my just-lit lamp, was Monnie.

She had her feet up on her pillows, and she'd dragged a quilt across her lap.

"Monnie!" I said, and my voice came out harsh 'cause I'd been so scared. "Monnie, why didn't you speak up when I came in?"

She laughed quietly. "You didn't even stop," she said. "Acted like the devil hisself was after you. I had to wait and see if the old coot followed you in that door. I ain't never seen him before. Wondered if he was coming after me."

I knew she meant to be funny, but I was mad— mad because I'd been so scared. I went over to her, tugged at her quilt, tightened it over her legs, not speaking.

"Want to set a spell?" she said. "Supper can keep. It's corn chowder. Want to keep me company?"

I sat on the floor near her feet, my arms clutched up tight around my knees, and I stared out the long window, not speaking because I was still mad at her. Scaring me that way!

Outside, an owl called, and I could hear the tree frogs singing away.

After a bit, Monnie said, "How do you think you'll make out?"

I didn't have to ask what she meant. "Fine!" I said, still angry. "Just fine and dandy."

"I think so, too," she said. "You got guts."

In my head, I said, *It takes more than guts, way more.*

"I think we should talk about it. No?"

"No!" I said.

"Well, we got to."

"Then, why'd you ask?" I said.

Monnie laughed. "Fair enough. But we got to talk. So let's talk 'bout these things in small snatches."

"I don't want to hear *any* snatches," I said.

Monnie put up a hand. "Just this for today and then I be done. We'll start with the easy things. Money. There's money in the kitchen. Behind the chimney box. And enough in the bank, too. I've saved most every penny from the mine insurance when your pa died and your grandpa, too. It's all there, growing big with interest."

I didn't answer, kept right on looking out the window. I even shifted a little, so my back was turned to her. If I couldn't stop her from talking, I could stop listening. I looked out the window, a fine night, the moon so bright there were shadows. And night creatures were already moving about, and . . .

"And there's bonds, too," she said. "They're in the strongbox at the bank. Had them made over in your name. You be careful, and there'll be enough till you're growed. I've saved almost every single cent from that insurance, and it's just been growing. Even bought ourselves some war bonds not long back. And . . ."

. . . and the deer were creeping silently from the

*woods, their legs like sticks among the trees at the edge
of the meadow, and . . .*

"And I'm telling you so you won't be worrying
over if you'll eat or have clothes and such," Monnie
went on softly. "And there'll even be money enough
for some treats. You needn't worry 'bout that. See?"

I didn't answer, couldn't answer, stared out at the
night, at the night creatures declaring that this time
was their own and . . .

I could hear the wheeze of Monnie's breath, feel
the weight of it in the air, hanging there, in and out,
in and out, and then it got stuck and lay on the air,
and she couldn't suck it in again. She made gaspy
sounds, and I breathed for her then. Nice and easy,
nice and easy, I breathed.

It took a moment, but then her breathing got
almost regular again, and she said, "I never seen you
so mad before."

"So? What do you expect?" I said.

"Don't suppose I'd expect much different,"
Monnie said then. "I knowed if'n it was me, I'd be
mad. Whooee! I'd be mad."

I turned and looked up at her.

She nodded at me. "Madder'n a wet hen."

I nodded. "Well, I am. I'm mad," I said.

We were both quiet then. Outside the frogs were

calling, and the owl hooting, and the crickets beginning their chirping, a spring sound, a summer
sound, but it was awful cold out still, yet it was
changing, summer would be here and . . .

And then, something welled up, something real,
physical, a choking feeling in my throat. "Monnie?"
I said.

She raised up her eyebrows.

But I just turned away, turned to the window
again. I listened to the fool frogs singing their fool
songs, same time as the owl was hooting that he's
out there looking to rip them up and eat them. And
still, they were singing.

I swallowed down the bones in my throat.

"Girl?" Monnie said. "Say it. Whatever."

I turned back to her. "Monnie?" I whispered.

But then, oh, God, I couldn't say this, couldn't.
Just inside my head, I said it, said the words.
Monnie, don't die, I said. *Please, please don't die.*

10

All I could think about in the days afterward was Monnie. Some days, I told myself she'd get better. Other days, I knew she was worse. Mostly she was worse. Her breathing was worse, and some days, she didn't even get out of bed till just before I got home from school. She pretended she'd been up all day. But I could tell. Once, as soon as I got home, I went in and felt the sheets and blankets on her bed, and they were still warm. But she hadn't said anything more, no more of those snatches of things she'd said we needed to talk about. And I was content to leave it that way.

It was the following week, a Wednesday, that I was in the library after school, looking for the *Life* magazine with the picture of the girl who had been bombed out of her house. I just wanted to see her face again. But I couldn't find it. Instead, I found a different magazine with a story that jumped right out at me. A new medicine had just been discovered, and it was being used to help soldiers who were hurt in the war. In the magazine, they called it a miracle drug, and they had pictures of these soldiers who had been saved by it—saved when they were almost given up for dead. A miracle, they called it. Could it be?

My heart began thumping hard. I wondered if Dr. Harkins had read about it. Did he know? Would it help Monnie?

I read it again. Yes, it was a miracle, and it could cure all sorts of wounds and infections and everything. I looked around the library. Nobody was watching. Quietly, carefully, I began ripping out the page.

I knew it was wrong. But I could come and put it back tomorrow. After I showed it to Dr. Harkins.

And then I remembered this was the day I had promised to talk to him.

Perfect.

Only one thing to do—go there. Right now. So I did.

Miss Cotter made an ugly face at me when I came in, her eyes squinted up. I didn't exactly blame her. Since I didn't want another scene, I smiled at her, real nice. And I said sweetly, "May I *please* talk to Dr. Harkins, *please?*"

She kept her eyes squinted up, and for a minute, she didn't answer. And then she said, "Sit! I'll go see."

She stood up. But she waited a minute to be sure I was seated before she started down the hall.

I chose a chair that faced down the hall, and I watched her go. Halfway there, she turned and looked back over her shoulder at me.

I motioned to her, a tiny wave of my hand.

She turned back and went to the end of the hall, and I saw her stop at one of the rooms there.

I looked around for the *Life* magazine, but it was gone.

After a while, Miss Cotter came and said, "It's all right. You can go in and see him now." She pointed. "His room is right down the hall."

Which, of course, I already knew.

But I said thank you, and went on down to his room, passing a lady with a tiny baby in her arms, on her way out.

Dr. Harkins was waiting for me at the door to his office, all smiles, smelling of his pipe, though it was nowhere to be seen. "I'm glad you kept your word," he said. "I've been looking forward to talking with you."

"Why?" I said, my heart suddenly leaping. "Did

you have something to tell me? About Monnie?"

He shook his head. "No, no," he said. "Just . . . just was looking forward to talking to you."

"Oh," I said. "Why?"

He shrugged. "I guess because—because your grandma's pretty sick. It must be hard for you."

"Yes," I said. "But . . . look at this!" I plopped my books down on his desk and pulled out the page from the magazine. "Do you know about this?" I said.

He sat down behind his desk and waved me to a seat in front of it. He glanced at the page. "Interesting, huh?" he said. "A whole new way of treating people."

"You already know about this?"

He nodded. "Oh, yes," he said. "Very promising."

"Do you have it?" I asked. "The medicine?"

"Penicillin?" he said. He shook his head. "It's not available to everyone yet. But we'll probably get it soon. It's mostly being used in the army."

"How soon?" I said.

"How soon, what?" he said.

"How soon can you get it?"

He shrugged. "Not sure." Then he frowned at me. "You're thinking of your grandma?"

I nodded.

He sighed. "Blessing," he said. "It won't help your grandma."

"How do you know that?" I said. "Last week, you said we needed a miracle. And here, it says so right here—miracle! Right there. It says so."

"It is a miracle," Dr. Harkins said quietly. "But it's not the kind of miracle that Monnie needs."

"How do you know?" I said. "You don't even have it. You said so. So how do you know? You can try it, can't you?"

Dr. Harkins leaned forward and picked up his pipe. He didn't light it or anything, just held it. "Blessing," he said, pointing it at the magazine page. "Look at this. Read it. It helps infection. It helps cure infections. You read it, right?"

I nodded.

"Monnie's problem isn't infection. It's her lungs, but mostly her heart. Her heart is plumb worn out, Blessing."

"What do you mean, worn out? It's . . ."

"Worn out," he said softly. "She has heart failure. That's why medicines won't help. Only a new heart would help her. And there's no way to get one of those."

Worn out. Monnie's heart was worn out. Monnie, who has the best heart.

I hadn't found the right miracle.

"Blessing," Dr. Harkins said. "It might be better if you just try and accept this. It's . . ."

"It's stupid, that's what it is!" I said, my voice so fierce I surprised myself. "It's really, really stupid."

"Yes, it is," he said. "It's really, really stupid."

"Then why don't you . . ." I looked up at him.

"Do something?" he said.

I nodded. "Yes! Why don't you do something?"

He sighed. "What would you have me do?" he said quietly. "Tell me what to do, and if I can, I'll do it."

I looked at him. "You will?" I said.

He nodded.

"Promise?" I said.

"Promise," he said.

"You'll get that medicine?" I said.

He sighed again. Then very quietly, he said, "I can try. I can try and get it. But . . ." He spread his hands and looked at me again.

But the medicine won't help. Monnie is dying. And that's the truth.

Tears welled up to my eyes. I blinked hard, pushed them down.

No.

Yes. Oh, yes. She is dying. You know it. You know it.

And just then, then I did know it. I did.

Monnie is dying.

I sucked in my breath, blinked hard, tried to concentrate on something else. I stared at the floor, the rug with its little worn circle right there by my feet.

Maybe Monnie had sat right here last week. Maybe she just nodded when he told her. Nothing we can do. Your heart is worn out.

I knowed that. Maybe that's what she said. *Yep, heart's plumb wore out.*

I stood up.

I picked up my book bag, hurried down the hall and out of the building. Then I began to run. I ran hard, my book bag slamming against my legs, ran and ran, till I was halfway up on the mountain. The sky was turning dark, a night sky coming down. I leaned against a tree, sobbing for breath, gasping. I was crying, didn't mean to cry, it was just happening, tears pouring down my face. I stood there for the longest time, leaning against the tree, crying, trying to catch my breath. After a while, I don't know how long, I quieted. I stood there breathing deep, listening to the sounds of the mountain around me—the doves cooing their mournful songs, the owls hooting their dismal question—*who, who?* I heard a coyote calling off in the distance, and after a bit, he was joined by another and then another, all of them setting up a dreadful, dismal howling. And it seemed to me then as if all of them, the owls and doves and coyotes, they weren't howling or hooting or calling. They were crying. All of us were crying.

11

Monnie was better. She was. I could see it. She had started getting up and moving around some, and one day when I came home from school, she was even outside in the garden. She didn't cough as hard, so maybe the cough medicine was helping. And as the days got warmer, the sun seemed to do her good, too. She'd sit on the porch with her Bible, reading and soaking up the warmth, and one day I noticed that two bright spots of pink had come to her cheeks. She even got herself down to church with me, two Sundays running. When she heard that Reverend Tucker was planning a special Easter Sunday service, inviting the town choir—that meant Jane!—and the town preacher up here to church, well, she told him she'd help out with the music. She said she'd play a special song, and I would sing, though we hadn't decided yet exactly what song we'd do.

As Monnie got better, I got better, too. Suddenly I found I was singing again. I hadn't planned to stop—it just seemed for a while that the songs had gone out of me. Now, though, I found myself walking around humming snatches of melody, and singing for the pure fun of it.

I hadn't forgotten that day with Dr. Harkins. Still, it could be a while before that happened. It could be a long, long while. Maybe Monnie thought so, too, because she hadn't gone back to any of those things she'd said we needed to talk about.

It was early on Easter morning, and Monnie and I were sitting on the porch talking about what music we'd do for ten o'clock service. The choir would do their regular singing. But Monnie and me were like an added attraction, so to speak. And we could do anything we liked. The sun was shining, and it seemed like spring was just about to burst.

"I think it should be 'The Old Churchyard,'" Monnie said. "Seems right, you think?"

I nodded. "I guess. But I'd rather something lively. Like 'Pretty Polly.'"

"And have Reverend Tucker think we're heathens?"

"Why not?" I said. "I think God likes happy music. Don't you?"

"Don't matter what I thinks," Monnie said. "It's what the reverend thinks. And he sets store by all them old sacred songs." Monnie turned to me then, worried-looking. "I jes' thought of something."

"What?"

"You. Wherever you go, you need music. You got to have a place where there's music."

"What do you mean—*where I go?*"

"Where you go live. After I'm gone."

"Monnie!" I said. "Don't start with . . ."

"Hush! Hush yourself now!" She put up a hand. "It's been a while. We need to talk 'bout these things. Who you going to live with? I been thinking and thinking on that. Can't live here by your lonesome."

I turned away, looked out over the railing at the rutted-up road that led down from the mountain. Live with someone? No, I was living here. With Monnie. Why was she starting again? Why now? It was a beautiful day, we were going to sing, everything was good. She was better. I didn't need to live with anybody. I'd be all grown up by the time she—died.

But . . . but I knew something was coming. And what if she was right? What if she died soon? Who would I live with? That thought had crept in my head a couple times, but each time, I'd pushed it away.

"Can't believe I forgot," Monnie said again. "And here, I thought I had it all fixed in my head. I picked out families for you. Thought maybe we'd talk 'bout which ones would suit. But I forgot music. I plumb forgot music."

"Stop it!" I said. "You've got time. You got lots of time."

"What you talking about, time?" she said. "Time's what I ain't got. And here, you could shrivel up and die without music. I got to think 'bout this again."

I was about to tell her to hush up when we both heard a car coming up mountain. People up here walk. So a car meant town people. Maybe the preacher? With Jane?

Monnie looked at me. "It's still far off," she said.

I nodded.

Up here on the mountain, you can hear things way before you see them. The air is so silent, so still, that some winter days you can hear snow falling from trees, or in fall, the leaves whispering their way to the ground. And now, early spring, you can actually hear the leaves budding out, little popping sounds like whispers of breath, when the leaf pods pop out of their covering.

"Probably the town church folks," Monnie said.

I nodded. It probably was. And that meant Jane

would be here soon. And Monnie would stop her mean talk.

I went to the edge of the porch, where I could see the road better, and leaned out over the railing. I couldn't see a car yet. But I did see a worm crawling across the bottom step, and I picked up a twig, slid it under him, and lifted him up. He dangled there in the air, wriggling frantically. It was cold where I stood, though, the step in shadow, so I moved back up again, holding the stick with the worm, and settled again by Monnie in the sun, still watching the road.

"Now, if I were your grampa," Monnie said, looking down the road, "I'd've had my shotgun out by now."

"You would? Why?" I asked.

Monnie smiled. "Why? 'Cause your grampa didn't set no store by town folks. I 'member one time, the town sheriff came up here looking for one of the Zooks. Your grampa sat here, right where I'm sitting this very minute. He waited till that car was almost out front. He eyed down the barrel of that gun. And began to shoot!"

"Did he *kill* him?" I asked.

Monnie made a face at me. "'Course he didn't kill him," she said. "Didn't mean to. Just scare him. And he did. When that sheriff hears that gun and sees the gravel, he turns his car around . . . well, tries to. Lordy, it was a sight. He tries to back and turn and back and turn, so crazy he runs right off the high road. He ends up with one tire hanging off into the gully."

Monnie paused, shaking her head and smiling.

"And?" I said.

She rocked back in her chair. "Oh, it was something!" she said. "He rights the car and gets it back on the road. And we see them little red rear lights hightailing it away. So just for fun, your grampa blowed one out! And that's the last we seen of that sheriff. He runned off like a dog with his tail between his legs and never come back up on this mountain again. Your grampa, he was real proud of hisself that day. And Ogden Zook, he just clapped your grampa on the back." She shifted in her rocker, smiling and nodding. "Those men knew how to take care of theirselves. And each other."

"Hillbillies," I said. It was such a mean, ugly word, and such a mean way it burst out of me, that I surprised myself. I didn't dare look at Monnie.

"What you say?" Monnie said. Her voice was level, calm. Quiet. But I knew very well she had heard what I said.

"Nothing," I said.

Why had I said that? Why had I said it that way? I felt so ashamed.

"Don't you never use that word again," she said.

I nodded.

"Answer me," she said.

"Yes, ma'am," I said.

"And you look at me when you speak to me."

I looked at her. The spots of color in her cheeks were even brighter. And her eyes were madder looking than I'd seen in a long, long time.

"Yes, ma'am," I said again.

She squinted up her eyes at me. "I don't care how bad you feeling," she said, very quiet-like, very calm. "Don't you give me mouth again. You hear?"

I nodded.

"You should be ashamed of yourself," she said. "Hillbillies, indeed! It's family up here. *Family.* Family that cares for each other." She got to her feet and started across the porch to the door.

At the door, she stopped and turned back to me. "What you doing with that worm?"

"Nothing," I said. "Just . . . watching it."

"Well, you let it go."

"Yes, ma'am."

"It's one of God's creatures. And don't you hurt it, neither. You hear?"

"Yes, ma'am," I said. I suddenly remembered how

when I was little, I used to cut worms in half and watch the two halves wriggle off. I always wondered if they ever got back together again, if they met their other halves. And if they recognized each other when they did.

She slammed the door behind her as she went in the house.

I went to the edge of the porch and, very gently, I let the worm down onto the ground. I wouldn't have hurt it. I hadn't cut up a worm since I was a little kid.

I stood there for a while, looking out over the railing, hoping to see whoever was coming up mountain. But there was no longer a sound of a car, so it must have turned in at the church.

Jane was probably there now. I could go down and see her. But somehow, I didn't want to. Didn't want to do any of the things that we were supposed to do today. Not even sing.

What I really wanted to do was go inside, find Monnie, and crawl into her lap. I wanted to pretend like I was a little kid again, like nothing was wrong, nothing was changed.

Like I hadn't turned into a nasty, mean person.

12

It was a long, slow walk to church that morning, the birds chittering at us from the treetops, the sun shining warm on our backs. On the north side of the trees and rocks, there were piles of snow, but in the sun, clumps of green were pushing through the bare earth, and you could see spring was just about ready to burst. Church is just down and around the curve, but it took a long time because Monnie had to keep stopping to rest. It was a nice walk, or could have been, except that Monnie was as silent as the grave. She was still mad at me, mad enough that she didn't even look at me, acting like I was invisible. Her lips were pursed up so that her mouth looked like one of those tobacco pouches when the string gets drawn tight.

Once, when we started up after a little rest, I asked

if I could carry the fiddle for her.

She shook her head. "Do it myself," she muttered, breathing hard.

"But it's heavy," I said.

"I don't know that?" she said.

I just shrugged.

She turned and went on, her back as straight as she could make it, her head high. And I knew if she had been able, she'd have trotted right away from me, wouldn't even have waited. So I just shut up my mouth. Which I probably should have done long ago.

When we finally got to the churchyard, people were bustling around, neighbors, as well as folks from the town choir. Folks were greeting each other, brushed and dressed up like I hardly ever see them. Some of the women sported new hats. "Bonnets," I heard Monnie mutter, scornful-like, under her breath. But she nodded at each person in her usual friendly way—lots friendlier than she was being with me.

Monnie didn't have a new bonnet, not a new anything. I didn't, either. Monnie and me, we don't go in for things like new Easter clothes. Only time I got new things was when school started every year. Not that I'd ever missed it much. But now, looking at folks, I thought maybe new shoes would have been nice. Edith and her sidekick Dorothy both had shiny new shoes—patent leather with flat bows. I tried not to look jealous, but I think I was. The colors of their dresses were wonderful, too, a rosy pink on Dorothy and a bright sun-yellow on Edith. They were both shivering because they had left their coats off, just to show off their new dresses. Dorothy had goose bumps all over her arms, and her teeth were kind of chattery. That made me feel a bit better.

Reverend Tucker stood in the vestibule in back with the town preacher, Reverend Hornby, greeting each family as they came in. I couldn't see Jane anywhere, though I knew she had to be here somewhere, probably in the choir room. But I could see that the church looked really special, all decked out with mountain flowers—laurel and crocuses and tall, spiky branches of yellow forsythia.

When Monnie and I stepped into the vestibule, both reverends came toward us. Reverend Tucker smiled and said hello to me in that kind of shy, quiet way he has. Then he took the fiddle from Monnie, took her by the arm, and led her off to the side, as if he wanted a private word with her.

That left me with Reverend Hornby. "The Lord is risen!" he said, smiling at me, throwing back his shoulders and sticking out his chest, as though he himself were responsible for the Lord's rising. "Hallelujah!"

Well. What was I supposed to say to that? So I said nothing.

It didn't seem to bother him that I hadn't answered. His eyes darted this way and that, looking for more newcomers, but nobody was coming up the steps, so he turned back to me. "I hear you're Jane's friend," he said.

I nodded again.

"She talks about you all the time," he said.

An evil little thought sped into my head—Jane telling me how he had dumped his dinner in the dog's dish. I smiled. "She talks about you, too," I said.

"I'm glad to hear it," he said quietly, his voice suddenly as soft and dismal as a mourning dove. "I know she's grateful to have a decent place to lay her head."

I almost choked on a laugh that came bubbling up. But I swallowed it down, and hoped my face didn't get as red as it felt.

Didn't matter. He wasn't paying any attention to me anymore. He had begun nodding and smiling at the Boltons, who had started up the steps beside me. Poppy was all brushed, his beard tucked tightly into his belt, and Mason was wearing a dress, something

I've only seen her do once before, at the funeral for the Marens' little boy who fell down a well shaft. She looked odd and stiff in it, and I had a sudden thought that this is how a daffodil might look if you tried to dress it. They both nodded at me, friendly-like, but didn't say a word, though that wasn't surprising.

"The Lord is risen!" Reverend Hornby boomed out. And I took that as my signal to get away. I quick scooted for the choir room, where I found Jane at the door, waiting for me, jiggling from foot to foot. She didn't have new clothes, but she was so smart and clean that you could almost feel the goodness just shining off her.

"You're here!" she said, and she hugged me. "I'm so glad." She nodded her head toward Reverend Hornby. "What'd he say to you?"

"He said," I said, and I tried to make my voice as dreary and dismal as his own. "He said you were grateful to have such a decent place with him."

"Dis-gusting!" she said.

"Uh-huh," I said. "And he told me you talk about me a lot. So I told him that you talk about him, too."

Jane just burst out laughing. "But guess what?" she said. "He's not all bad. We're having an Easter egg hunt later in the churchyard in town. And there's candy and eggs and everything."

"Wow. Lucky you," I said.

"Maybe you could come?" she said.

I shook my head. Not with the way Monnie was today.

"Any candy I find," she said, "I'm going to give to Johnny and Buck."

"What?" I said. "Are they going to be there?"

She shook her head. "No, silly. I mean, I'll save it for them." She smiled at me. "I got to tell you something, though."

"What?" I said.

"Where can we talk?" she said.

I looked around the church. It was filling up fast, but the clock said we still had twenty minutes before service began. "Want to go outside?" I said.

Jane nodded. "Yeah."

We hurried outside, past the people coming in twos and threes, big families with children, and sometimes—mostly—women alone. Everyone looked so shiny and clean that again I wished I had something new to wear. I wondered what was happening to me. I never used to care about things like this.

We found two boulders under a cottonwood tree, facing the sun.

As soon as we'd gotten settled, Jane leaned forward, tugging a piece of her hair that had come loose from her braids. "Know what?" she said. "I get to see my pa in a week. And Buck and Johnny, too. The family they're with is bringing them to meet us at Pa's house. My old house."

"Next week?" I said.

She nodded, and her eyes were bright. I thought how pretty she looked, especially now that she was all brushed up and clean. It was really rotten that she'd been taken from her pa. But there were some good things about it—like having decent clothes and her teeth fixed.

"One week from today," she said. She clasped her hands together in her lap. "I can't wait."

"Do you know how they are? How's Buck?"

"They say he's fine. But I can't wait to see him. Both of them."

"Does that mean you're going back home?" I asked. "Will you all stay?"

She shook her head. "No. Miss Cotter said no. But I think we can soon. If not next week, sometime soon. I bet."

I thought then of what Monnie had said to me that morning—about needing to find someone to take care of me. Maybe she was right. What if I got someone like Reverend Hornby? But I wouldn't think about that now. I wouldn't.

"We can't be there alone, though," Jane went on, making a face. "Old Cotter will be there the whole time. But I don't even care. I just can't wait to see my pa and Johnny and Buck." She sighed. "I worry about Buck so much. Miss Cotter says he's okay. But I don't know. Do you think he's getting his medicine? You know, for his seizures?"

"Sure he is," I said.

"But I bet they don't know how to predict them like I can. You know, I can tell ahead of time if he's going to have an attack."

"I bet they know," I said. "He's okay. They're both okay. And in just a week, you can see for yourself."

Jane nodded. But the happy look she had had just a minute ago was gone.

"I bet he's okay," I said again.

"How do you know?" she said. She didn't say it in a mean way—just sort of sad-like.

"I just do," I said.

I was going to say that's why they took him away. But then it seemed like I'd be saying Jane wasn't a good enough mother. So I just didn't say anything.

We were both quiet. I looked around at the sun shining hot on us; the trees swelling into bloom; the movement of two tiny birds above us, hopping from branch to branch, the branches trembling under their twin weight. I listened to their soft chirping and tweeting, to the song of the frogs off in the pond.

All of it was beautiful, sweet and spring-like and—new! It should have filled me with happiness. But it didn't. All I could think of was Monnie. She was sick. She was talking about dying again. And I had been mean to her.

I looked again at Jane. She pointed to a brown creeper scurrying in his funny, upside-down way along the tree trunk beside us. "Don't you just love spring?" she said softly.

I nodded. And then I blurted out, "Monnie's mad at me."

"How come?"

"I said something stupid."

Jane laughed. "So? I always say stupid things."

"But this was *really* stupid," I said.

The church bells began ringing suddenly. I clapped my hands over my ears, but Jane stood up and held out a hand to me, pulling me to my feet.

"Come on," she said. "They'll be looking for us."

We started into church together. At the doorway, I could see Mrs. Hatch, the choir director, looking out. She beckoned to us, hurrying us along.

"Don't worry," Jane said. "Monnie will get over it. Grown-ups forget."

I nodded but didn't answer. She was probably

right. Monnie would get over it—eventually. And now it was almost time for the music. But with Monnie mad at me, and me all squirrelly and anxious with her—well, how in the world would we ever make good music together?

13

We didn't make good music. Monnie and me, we just didn't get together in the music at all. Even in "The Old Churchyard," it was like she was playing one song and I was singing another entirely. The whole time, I felt shy and awkward, and my voice quavered in spots and seemed flat and dull, even to my ears. I remembered that night at Ellie's, when I had forgotten about being shy and sang to the folks there, to Monnie, to the Martins and to the baby yet to be born, even to the coyotes, and the mountain. I tried to get that feeling back, that way of forgetting everything but the music. But I couldn't. All I could think about was Monnie, and how mad she was at me. Also, the town choir didn't sing at all well with our choir. And the two preachers could have been talking about two different Gods. Reverend Tucker told about the God who cared so much that He gave us His only Son. And Reverend Hornby told how God's son had to die for our sins and how He would punish sinners with fire and hell. It was like no two people in that whole church were in tune with what any other two people were saying or doing or even singing.

Afterward, Monnie said it all came from having town people up in the first place. And to make it worse, I had hardly two minutes to spend with Jane in the church hall afterward. Her choir packed up so quick, they didn't even stop for the cakes the ladies had made, because they were having their own Easter egg hunt in town.

It was just a miserable day, and I was glad when it was over. It was nighttime, and we had had supper, and I was sitting by the fire with my book, when Monnie said, "I been thinking 'bout music and where you'll go live. Don't know where we can find music for you."

I didn't answer.

"Nobody really got good music but you and me," Monnie said. "Think you can make music on your own?"

"No!" I said. "I can't make music, and I can't sing without you. And I won't. So there. So stop talking about it."

Monnie just burst out laughing, that hooting kind of laugh that made me so mad. "Why, of course you'll make music, girl!" she said. "'Course you'll sing. How could you not?"

I glared at her, but I didn't say anything more.

"You'll probably do all right," Monnie said. "Maybe you can join up with the church choir."

I shrugged. I was not going to talk about this. I just was not.

"So listen," Monnie said. "This is what I think. There's the Boltons. Poppy and Mason are good folks. And there's the Cravens . . ."

The Cravens!

"Monnie, stop!" I said. I didn't even look up from my book. "Stop. I'm not living with anyone."

"What you going to do?" she said. "Wait for that Cotter wolf to gobble you up?"

"I don't need anyone. I can live . . . I can live alone. And anyway, you're not dying. But if something happens, I'm okay—alone. Right?"

"Maybe someday. Not now, though. Not by a long shot."

"So?" I said. "I'll figure it out someday, all right?" I went back to my book. I had finished *Little Women* and was reading another book Miss Ford had lent to me—*The Secret Garden*. I'd already read it once and was reading it a second time. It was just as good the second time, maybe even better.

"We got to figure it out now," Monnie said. "'Cause only God knows when it will happen. But I can tell you, it will be soon enough. So you listen up. Like I said, there's the Boltons. They're good folks. They'll treat you good. Or there's the Cravens. More good folks. Of course, they got so many children." She stopped. "You listening? Let go of that book!"

The Boltons? They had Child—that strange, half-baby, half-child who is so creepy. And besides, they never talk, don't say a word, and Mason is more like a man than a woman, not at all like a mother or anything—not that I've ever had a mother, not that I remember anyway. And the Cravens . . .

I closed the book. "I'm listening!" I said. But that didn't mean I had to let her words get inside of me. I began making music in my head, a busy bee-like kind of humming to shut out the bad things she was saying.

She frowned at me. "Then there's the Hollisters, more good folks. Only thing there is, they don't got enough money to feed their scraggly dogs, much less their own selves and you, too. So even though you'd bring money, I think we got to cross them off. You think?"

I nodded. But still, I didn't answer. How could she

talk like this—all calm, and sensible, like we were making a grocery shopping list? Inside, I made the music louder, a noisy music, lots of drums added in.

But then, I couldn't help thinking about something. "What about if they don't want me?" I asked.

"Oh, they want you," she said. "No worry about that. We talked."

"What?" I stared at her. "You talked to them already? Without asking me?"

"I'm asking you right now," she said. "The Boltons. The Cravens. And I got another, but it worries me."

"Why? Who?"

"The Alley people. They're good enough. But they's town folks."

She looked hard at me then, frowning. And I knew she was remembering this morning and what I had said.

I just looked away.

"Can't see you living down in town," Monnie went on. "You're us. Mountain people."

I am mountain people. Even if I sometimes said mean things.

"So, talk to me," Monnie said.

"Talk about what?" I said. "I don't want to live with any of them."

I want you.

"Well, you think on it," she said. "And let me know. I got to write it down at the bank, make it all nice and legal. Else, that Cotter wolf will have her claws in you faster than you can blink."

"Can I read now?" I said.

"Go on," she said. And she waved a hand at me.

I turned back to my book, to Colin and Mary and Dickon. Oh, I do love Dickon. And that robin with the key, and the hidden garden, the walls all covered with vines.

But Monnie had spoiled it all—again. She always spoiled things, talking about dying. Why couldn't she just let things be? She had started all sorts of bad thoughts in my head—who would I live with? Live with, and leave all this—Monnie, my house—all this?

I looked up at her then, because I heard her grunt or groan or something. She was bent over, reaching for something on the floor, her fiddle.

"What do you want?" I said. "Can I get it?"

"I can do it," she said. And she reached out further—but then, just like that, she fell—tumbled right out of her chair onto her hands and knees.

I jumped up. "Monnie!" I said. I reached for her, tried to stop her fall. But she slid away from me, sprawled face down right there on the floor.

"Monnie?" I said again.

Nothing. She didn't answer.

I bent over her. "Here," I said. "Let me help you. Are you okay? What happened?"

She shook her head. "Just a little dizzy spell. Here, help me up."

I grabbed under her arms, pulled at her.

But I couldn't move her, couldn't get her up.

I rolled her over partway, so that her face was up. She was pale, real pale, but for those two bright spots of pink.

"Monnie!" I said, and my throat was so tight, I could hardly speak. "Monnie, what happened?"

"Nothing big. Just bent too far, I guess. Got a little dizzy."

"Can you get up?" I said.

She nodded, and I slid my hands under her arms and again tried to lift her. But she was heavy and it was really hard to do.

"Let me be," she said, after a bit. "Let me rest here. I'll get up in a minute. Don't fuss. I'm all right."

But she had closed her eyes, and her breathing was funny, coming in little spurts. Breathe. Pause. Breathe again. Long pause.

"What can I do?" I said. "Tell me what to do."

"Nothing," she said. "Just sit here with me."

"Can I get you something?"

"A blanket."

"Right here? On the floor?"

She didn't answer.

I took the big quilt off her bed, then hurried back to where she lay on the floor. I tucked the blanket tight around her, then realized her head was flat against that cold floor. I went back to her room, got a pillow, then slid it under her head. Then I sat down on the floor beside her. One of her hands lay outside the covers on the linoleum. I picked it up and it was cold, so I tucked it under the blanket.

"I'm fine," she said after a moment. "Just a little dizzy spell."

"Can you get up yet?" I said.

"No. Just let me rest."

So I did. But my heart was beating so hard, so furiously, I thought it would jump right out of my chest. For the longest time we stayed there, Monnie breathing in that funny way. And then I realized that she was sweating, too, her forehead suddenly all damp and wet.

I took an edge of the quilt blanket and wiped her forehead.

She smiled, but she still didn't open her eyes. "You're a good girl," she said softly. "A real good girl."

But I wasn't a good girl. Not at all. I said bad things, and I made fun of Monnie's stories. I wouldn't listen when she talked and tried to make plans for me. And when we made music together this morning, I couldn't even make good music with her. I wasn't good. Nothing was good. Everything was wrong. And if there was a God in His heaven, like those preachers were talking about, I sure didn't know what He was up to.

14

Monnie had lain on the floor half the night, with me sitting beside her, before she'd felt able to get up and move into her bed. And in the two weeks since, she hadn't been right, I knew that. Her breathing was more raggedy, and she got quiet, hardly talked at all. But the biggest change was that there was no more music. And that about broke my heart.

I tried to help her more, by making meals and such, though I'm a terrible bad cook. About all I could make was eggs and toast and cheese grits. And then after we ate, I'd read to her from *The Secret Garden*. She listened and even nodded in places, but I could see it cost her, see that she just wanted to go to sleep. She was so quiet, so far away, that she scared me.

I thought and thought and thought. And though

it made me feel all shaky inside, I began to realize I had to do something. I couldn't keep on fooling myself. Maybe I would need a place to live. Bad things were coming. And one thing Monnie had said was right—about that Cotter wolf. I did not want her messing in my life, doing to me what she'd done to Jane. I'd even seen her in school one day, talking to Miss Ford in the hallway. And from the way they looked at me as I went by, I just knew they were talking about me. What if she was already nosing around, knowing Monnie might die?

Monnie had laid out some names of folks I could go with. I knew them all. I even liked them—but enough to live with? I didn't know. Because some folks, they look all sugary on the outside, but when they don't know you're looking, you find things out. Like with Jane and the preacher.

So, after tons of thinking and even praying, I began to make myself a plan. If I had to live with someone, I would find out about them first. I would go and spy, look in their houses at night. Of course, I couldn't let Monnie know what I was doing. Even though she wanted me to have a place all set, she might be mad at me for spying, especially on neighbors. But how else could a person know what was what? So I figured once Monnie was in bed and asleep—and she'd been going to sleep earlier and earlier—then I'd go on outside. I'd slip across the mountain, or down into town, and I'd look in windows. When it's dark and the lights are on and curtains or shades not drawn, a person can tell a lot by what she sees.

So on a bright, moon-filled night, about a week later, I started my plan. I waited till the square of light from Monnie's window had blinked out. I dressed warm, and I slipped out into the dark. I had decided to start with the Boltons 'cause they're the closest. They live just up mountain from us, so it would be an easy walk in the dark. I walked up the rocky, rutted road from our place to theirs, feeling my way, knowing the ground under my feet as well as I know my own front yard. Neighbors up here, we don't horn in on one another, but we do get together, so I'd been up here plenty. And one thing I knew, before I even tiptoed up onto their porch that ran around three sides of that house high on the hill, was this: The Boltons are a mighty queer bunch. I think in all the time I've known them, the only time I've heard more than a word or two from Mason or Georgie is at Ellie's when they sing. And they only sing once in a blue moon.

There are four of them. There's the mama, Mason; the papa, called Poppy, who used to give me lollipops when I was little; and an old, old lady called

Georgie. There's also that strange child who they just call Child.

I paused, my heart thudding hard. Could I really live with them? Live without Monnie? I felt a lump come up in my throat, and I blinked back tears. I thought about God, about all He'd given me. And I thought about all He was taking away now. But I couldn't pray. It was too late for prayers. Or even tears. Monnie wouldn't be all right. She was going to die. And I had to find a place to live.

I had a plan, and I promised myself I'd carry it out. But still, I couldn't quite make myself move up onto that porch. And then, even though I had just told myself it was too late for prayers, I couldn't help praying again. *Please, God, please. I won't ask for much in a new family. Not even that they have music. But maybe—maybe, you could just let Monnie live awhile longer?*

I looked around me at the night, at the stars hanging there so close, they seemed to tangle in the branches of the trees. Some nights, it seems like God does hear when I talk to Him like that. Sometimes, He even sends something to answer me—a shooting star, the call of a coyote, something that says: I'm here, I'm listening to you. But this night He didn't say a word.

I crept up on the porch, and the old dog Oscar

suddenly came around a corner, snapping at my heels like he'd bite them off. But Oscar knew me, and it didn't take much to shush him up. I just lay a hand on his head, patted him softly. "Nice doggie," I whispered. "Good doggie. Hush now." And he did.

I tiptoed close to a long, low window, crouched down, and peered in. I saw the kitchen with candles burning on a table, and what looked like a kerosene lamp on the mantel. I had forgotten! I think they're the only people on the mountain who don't have electricity. How could I live like that? I'd told God I wasn't going to ask for much—but no electricity?

Through the window, I could see Mason by the black iron stove, stirring something in a pot so big you could put a whole entire hog into it. Next to her, Poppy was snoogling up to her. As I watched, I saw him put one paw right on her big fanny.

She turned and yelped, and even through the glass, I heard her. And then she swatted him.

But I saw that they were both laughing. I also saw something else—neither of them had any teeth. Another thing I'd forgotten. If they had enough money, like Monnie said, why not get their teeth fixed? Come to think of it, Georgie had no teeth either.

Poppy gave Mason another tweak on her bottom, and then he went and settled himself in a rocking chair by the fire. He picked up a shoe, and began doing something with it, stitching it, looked like.

For a long while, I watched. And all that time, neither of them spoke to the other. But they seemed comfortable, quiet and nice and kind of . . . well, kind of boring, actually. But then, they were old. So I couldn't expect much else. And they weren't fighting, and they weren't yelling. And best of all, they weren't drinking—like Jane's papa. I didn't see Georgie anywhere from where I stood, but as I watched, suddenly, Child came into the room. She crept in on all fours, just like a baby, though she must have been five years old already. Her hair hung down to the floor on either side of her face, as she came forward, moving like a little crab across the floor. She crept up to Poppy and stopped. He dropped the shoe he'd been working on, leaned down, then swept her up in his arms and set her on his lap.

She leaned her head against his chest, like she was going to rest a moment. And then, after a minute, she sat up and put her hands on either side of his head. She just held his head in her hands a minute. And then, real slow, she began running her little hands up and down his face, across his eyelids, to his ears and his hair, then back to his face again. I looked from them to Mason. She was paying them no mind, was just stirring her huge pot of whatever, and I turned to watch Child and Poppy again. Child was still doing that touching, playing, seeming to be memorizing his face, almost.

I don't know how long they did that, or how long I stood at the window watching. Poppy just held still as a spider, and that child kept on playing her fingers over and over on his face.

There was something hypnotic about it, like watching a magic lantern show. The candlelight was flickering around them, and they were so still, and Poppy was letting that child play her fingers over his face. Poppy was so patient, so silent. And Child was silent, too. Yet suddenly, I realized something—they were talking to one another. With her fingers, that child was telling him something. And he was listening as hard as she was speaking. It did something to my heart, something good, and sad at the same time, sort of melancholy. And then, I don't know what came over me, but suddenly, I felt tears come to my eyes. And yet I watched. For the longest time, Child kept on touching his face, his hair, and his ears. And Poppy held still for her. I wondered what they were saying to one another. For some reason then, I began to feel lonesome, and I wished like anything that I had someone who would—well, not *do* that, but would *listen* like that. I mean, Monnie listens. But—this was different.

After a while, I turned away, and crept down from the porch, almost tripping over old Oscar, who had plopped himself down right behind me. I wiped my sleeve across my face, and I heard my breath go out in a little *whoosh*, like a sigh—and I realized I'd been holding it without even knowing I was doing it.

I stood for a moment, thinking about what I'd just seen. They were different. They weren't like Monnie. They had no electricity. And no teeth. But there was something there.

I remembered then what I'd been thinking of before, about God. I looked around again at the stars, the moonlight, the night. And I told God, *All right. Maybe you did answer me, maybe you did. Because there was something there to warm your heart.*

There was.

15

Scary as it was, I knew I had to keep looking for places to live. Monnie surely wasn't getting any better. And there were fits of coughing, when you could just tell she was getting worse. So I had to look at all the places Monnie had suggested. I decided to wait for the weekend, though. The day after the Boltons, I'd been so tired I could hardly keep my eyes open in school. So the following Friday night, I waited till after Monnie was asleep. This would be a long, long walk, so I dressed real warm, coat and gloves and boots, and then I tiptoed out, heading for the Cravens' place.

The stars shone hard and cold, as I walked carefully down our side of the mountain to the fork in the road. Then I started up the other side, leaning forward into the hill, taking big, deep breaths of the night air. I smelled musky smells, like skunk and weasel, and even a bear somewhere.

The moon hung low, full and round. I thought of the story Monnie tells about the man in the moon. She said a man was out once on a Sunday gathering wood when he met an angel. The angel asked why he wasn't resting on Sunday, and he said he never rested on Sundays. So the angel sent him to the moon as punishment, where he would work all the time. Monnie says if you look real close on nights of the full moon, you can see a stick of wood on his shoulder.

This night, I couldn't see the stick of wood. But I did see him smiling. If he's being punished, it seems to me he's pretty happy about it.

It took a long time to reach the top of the mountain, where about a dozen houses are strung out, each high on its own little hillock, looking over the road.

The moon had dipped behind a cloud, and the light was dimmer, but still bright enough to see by. Very carefully, I took myself up the rickety path to the Cravens' house, slow step by slow step, trying to be quiet and not wake anyone.

There's a whole pack of Cravens, all girls. There's Essie Mae, who's in my class, when she comes to school, which isn't that often. There's her sister, Allie

Mae, one grade lower. There's her little sister, Anna Mae, two grades lower. There's the twins, Ella Mae and Missy Mae, in kindergarten. And there's a whole mess of littler ones at home, whose names I don't know. But I bet they're all named something-Mae. Seems that mama has no imagination when it comes to names.

I crept onto the porch and peered in the first window I came to, my face pressed against the glass.

It took a minute, trying to focus in the dark. But then I saw the mama and papa lumped together in one bed, and alongside, a cradle. I couldn't see over the sides of the cradle, so I didn't know for sure how many babies were there, but I bet more than one. On the floor was their old dog, Moxie, big as a horse almost, but it, too, was sound asleep, didn't move an inch. It hadn't even cocked an ear when I came to the window, so maybe it had gotten deaf or something.

I watched for a long while, but nothing in that room moved. Could have been dead, the way they slept so still. But this I could see: they had beds to sleep in, and sleeping they were doing, not stretched out drunk on the floor, and not slumped over in a chair. So that was good. And with the moonlight peeping in, and everyone so still, it seemed peaceful-like.

I backed away, tiptoed to the next window, and peeked in there. And there I saw the biggest mess of children I have ever seen. There were three beds in the room, lined up in a row, and children in them, two and three to a bed. Some had their heads to the top, some to the bottom, so that their feet were right in each other's faces. In one bed, three little ones were lumped together in the center, like puppies who just got tired out and fell asleep in the middle of playing. I tried counting heads, but in the darkness, I just couldn't be sure. I thought there were nine, but when I counted a second time, I came up with ten. I just stood there shaking my head.

If I came here, I'd sure bring my own bed. And I wouldn't share it, either. Sometimes a person has got to be alone, and sleeping is one of those times. Then I had another thought—if I did have to come here, it would be because Monnie wasn't needing her own bed anymore. Maybe I could bring that, too, as part of my dowry, so to speak.

I swallowed down the feeling in my throat that always came when I thought like that about Monnie. I fixed my mind on that bed, instead, thought about how one of the little girls would like a bed of her own.

I watched for a long time, but not one of those children moved. Good thing, too, 'cause one move would surely wake up all the others in the bed. There were some things to be noted, though. There were beds and all the family were in the beds. And was it just my imagination—or did they all seem peaceful and nice? Though I guess most people seem peaceful when they're asleep.

I stood for just another moment longer, then tiptoed round to the next room and peered in the window there. It was a kitchen, and though it was dark inside, it seemed to be tidy, things nice and cleared up, no dirty mess left in the sink or on the tables.

I tiptoed around the house to the back. The yard was neat, a small garden turned over, a fence round it to keep out deer and pesky rabbits. Also, I saw an empty wash line—and that was good, no wash left hanging on the line overnight to get frozen or rained or snowed on.

I took a deep breath, then came back to the porch, and peeked in all the windows one more time. Everyone was still sleeping, even the dog, nice and peaceful. The yard was good, the wash line good, the house was cared for and . . . and I couldn't help thinking how many people there were here, so many of them! I didn't have even one sister or brother. How would I manage with ten or more of them? I mean, it could be a nice, friendly feeling, like always having company in the house. But then again, it could be awful. There'd be no privacy at all, and I bet every person, even the kids in that house, had to be bothered to death with taking care of littler ones.

Still . . . still, it might be a place I could lay my head if need be. Especially if I brought my own bed to lay it in.

It was late then, the moon hidden in clouds, the wind whistling softly around the corners of the house, and I suddenly realized I was shivering fiercely in the night cold. It was time to go home. I had done what I came to do. I turned and tiptoed down from the porch and hurried away, my hands dug deep in my pockets, my shoulders hunched against the cold. And as I walked, I started doing something I knew full well I shouldn't—I began to pray. I had given up on regular prayers because it was too late for that. But as I hurried home, I suddenly thought: Why not pray for a miracle? I knew God doesn't usually grant miracles to the average, ordinary person. Take the Boltons. They're stricken with that child who can't talk nor walk. But does God reach down and make that little one well? No. In the Bible stories, He made lame people walk and blind people see, and did all sort of tricks. But that was long ago, when He still had to prove who He was. Now He just sits up there, and though He talks to you once in a while, He doesn't interfere. And I always believed that's how it should be.

I thought different now. I needed a miracle, just like Dr. Harkins said. And so, all the way home, I prayed harder than I've ever prayed. I said all the prayers I've ever learned, the ones I learned from Monnie, the ones I learned in Sunday school. I said Now I Lay Me Down to Sleep, and I said the Grace before meals. And then I began the Our Father— and I stopped. *Thy will be done.* That's what that prayer said. *Thy will be done.* But I didn't want God's will. Not if He was planning on taking Monnie from me.

But then, what if His will was that Monnie should live? I didn't know. But I couldn't risk it. So I skipped over that prayer.

I still had a long ways to go before I was home, so I said all those prayers a second time, and then a third time. And when I was finished, well, I found myself just talking to God regular, the way I always do. Sometimes I think that if others heard, they might think I was bold, talking like God's just a normal person. I figure He understands, though. So what I said was this: "Lord, I know how busy You are. You have to oversee this whole world, even over to China and those places. So maybe You haven't noticed particularly what's going on here. Well, you know how Monnie's not just my mama? She's my mama and my papa and everything—my whole family, all rolled in one. She's aunts and uncles and cousins. I don't have any others, not like the Cravens with their hordes of little ones. There's just Monnie and just me. But now Monnie's sick, really, really sick. Did You know that? And Dr. Harkins says we need a miracle. I know it's probably not fair asking You. Probably everybody asks for that. But isn't this different? Just a little miracle, but it would be a big one for me. So please grant me this one thing. And so, that's all, Lord." I took a deep breath and swallowed hard. And then I added, "But Lord, if . . ."

But I couldn't say the rest of the words, the words Monnie taught me. I knew I should say them—*If it's not in Your plan, then Thy will be done.* But I couldn't say those words. And I really did try. Finally I found some words, other words, different ones. Maybe not as good, but the best I could do. I whispered them, fighting back the tears that were suddenly welling up in me. "But if that's not in Your plan, Lord, then . . . well then, Lord, I'll try to understand. Amen."

I looked up at the sky, the stars, at Orion blazing overhead, all those things God had made. They were miracles, weren't they? All around us were miracles, the flowers, the snow, the mountain, babies being born.

There were miracles all over the place. I just needed one more, my very own. Maybe He would do it, give me the one thing I really, really needed.

And I figured there was nothing wrong with praying for that.

16

It must have been way past midnight when I finally crept into the house. I took off my outdoor things and put them away, then stopped quietly by Monnie's door the way I'd gotten in the habit of doing lately, listening for her breathing.

Our house is *really* little. We have this one big room for living and reading and eating. To one side of that is a room for Monnie, and next to that is a kind of added-on room for me. That's it but for the closet for the toilet, an indoors one, too. In that little house, Monnie's breathing was so loud I could have been inside my own room with the door shut tight and pillows stuffed up at the crack, and I still would have heard. Suddenly though, her breathing eased, like it does sometimes after she's been holding still a while, not walking, not exerting herself even to put on her slippers. She began to breathe in and out, nice and sweet. And I thought: *Good. She'll rest quietly now, at least for a while.*

"'Night," I whispered, but not out loud, just to myself, sort of like a blessing.

"That you?" Monnie said. "Come on in, why don't you?"

It was so sudden the way she spoke, that I was startled.

"You awake?" I said.

"I'm awake," she said. And she patted the bed beside her.

Did she know I'd been out? Or did she think I was just wakeful?

I went into her room, but I didn't climb in bed with her. Just a few weeks ago, a month or more, I had climbed in with her. But she seemed too frail now, like just my moving around would set off her coughing. Also, she'd be sure to feel the cold coming right off me—the outdoor cold. So I pulled over the chair from the corner, the chair that the moon sits in, pulled it up close to her bed. I mussed my clothes around a little while I did, so it might look like I'd just fallen asleep with my clothes on.

"How come you're still awake?" I said.

"I been thinking," she answered.

"Thinking what?" I said.

"Thinking about the night you was born," she said.

"Why that?" I said. "That was a long while ago."

"Don't know," she said. "Just thinking lots of things lately. Thinking about your grampa, too. And your mama. All sorts of things."

My mama. How I wished she was here now. I squinted up my eyes, thinking, trying to picture her. I've tried that for so long, years and years. I was only two when she died, but sometimes, I think I can see her—or sense her. I think I remember a soft blue dress and a teddy bear in her lap and yellow hair, and I remember how she smelled of soap. But then, I think, I don't really remember her. I just remember because in that one picture I have of her, she's holding me in her lap and I'm holding a teddy bear. Still I have that sense of the way she smelled, how soft she was, how she held her arms around me.

"Oh, you was something else when you was born," Monnie went on. "Ellie was here, helping your mama get you borned. After you was finally here, Ellie put you in my arms, and I jes' looked down at you, and then I looked at Ellie and I said, 'Now, how come I got me such a ugly little baby?' And we laughed and laughed. 'Cause you was about the prettiest baby anybody's ever seen. You was really something else. Clear, pale skin, those huge eyes, still huge they are. And you looked so—knowing. Right off, you looked round this very room, like you knew all about it. You wasn't a baby who slept much. But you didn't cry, neither. You just looked at everything, took it all in. You was so extra-special beautiful. Ellie said God was giving your mama a special gift. Here was your mama, your papa killed in the mine, and she'd be needing to raise you on her own. So He made you extra special."

I smiled. I'd heard this story many times. But I always liked hearing it again. Though I always wondered how come if I was a beautiful baby, I got to be so ordinary looking now. I said that to Monnie once, and she just said, You wait and see. You just wait and see.

Well, I've been waiting a long while. But I didn't say anything about that now.

Monnie was quiet for a long time, and I thought maybe she'd fallen asleep. But then she went on, and her voice was different, far-off, like she was answering a question, though I hadn't said anything. She said, "Your mama?"

"What?" I said.

There was a long pause, a long shaky breath, and then Monnie laughed. "Oh," she said. "Your mama, she was so in love with you. From the first second she saw you. And know something? Something odd happened to me when you was born."

"What?" I said. Because though I had heard this story many times, I'd never heard about anything odd.

There was another long pause. And then Monnie said, "Looking at you there in my arms, something comed over me, though for a long time, I didn't know what to call it."

She breathed deep a few times, almost panting. And then she went on, "See, 'fore you got here, I weren't sure at all what I'd think of you. I was pleased enough a baby was on the way, but lotsa babies get borned every day. And truth is, I didn't feel nothing toward you at all 'fore you got here."

Monnie took a deep, shaky breath then, like she was trying to get air deep down into her lungs. And then she spoke again. "Awe," she said, finally. "That was odd. The feeling I got when I seen you. Awe."

Awe? Is that really what she'd said? It wasn't a word I even thought she knew. Or was it "Aw!" she meant, like "gosh" or "golly"?

"Awe?" I said.

"Awe," she said quietly. "Yes, awe. Just like love, only more better. Maybe it's what I'll feel when I see God. And maybe that's what you was. A piece of the Almighty. This tiny, perfect person. And then, see, don't know how I knew, but I knew. Sudden like, I got this feeling—your mama, she'd be gone in no time at all. Which is jes' what happened. And then you came to be mine to care for. All mine. And awe and love has kept me going all these years."

Monnie stopped, breathing deeply. Then she put out a hand and lay it on top of mine, which was lying on her covers. "Where you been?" she said.

"Been?" I said.

"You been out," she said.

I sucked in my breath.

"Yes," I said.

"Doing what?"

Thoughts raced around like little mice inside my head. I wanted to lie. Had to lie. I couldn't tell her what I'd been doing. I mean, I knew she wanted me to choose a place. But I just couldn't tell her that I was doing that—getting ready for her to die. Spying on neighbors? How could I tell her that?

"Just outside," I said. "You know. Out."

"Doing what?" she said again.

"Nothing," I said. "Just, you know, looking. At the stars, the night creatures."

"Heard you was up at the Boltons other night."

I sucked in my breath. I was startled, scared even. Who had seen me? Who had told Monnie?

Monnie chuckled softly. "No secrets on this

mountain, you should know that. So what was you doing?"

"Looking!" I said. The word just burst out of me. I felt tears well up. "Looking! Trying to see what they're like, what it would be like to live with them."

"That's good," Monnie said softly. "That's real, real good."

"And I peeked in at the Cravens tonight!" I went on. "They have so many children! I don't know . . . ." I stopped and shook my head.

"I know," Monnie said. "Might be real hard with all them little ones."

"I just don't know," I said. "I just don't know." And by then, tears were running down my face.

"You'll figure it out," Monnie said. She patted my hand, over and over, her hand so light, no more than a whisper or a cloud. "You will. Before I go, you'll have figured it out. Don't fret." She kept patting my hand, hers feeling so light and thin, as though the bones in her hand were already fading, thin and whispery-like.

I couldn't answer, my voice stuck tight in my throat.

"I been trying to figure things, too," Monnie said softly. She turned her head and looked at me.

"You have?" I whispered.

"This feeling—awe, love? You think that's enough?"

"What do you mean?" I said.

Monnie kept her face turned to mine. And in the moonlight, I thought her eyes were wet. "I've wondered 'bout that," Monnie said softly. "Did I give you enough? You think?"

Yes, you did! I nodded. But I couldn't say the words. I couldn't, couldn't squeeze them past the tears that were pushing their way up my throat. I tried, opened my mouth, then closed it up. But still, the words were stuck inside. I just lay my head down on the bed, right on top of Monnie's hand that was holding my hand. I pressed it hard. *Yes!* I said inside my head. *Yes, Monnie, yes, you gave enough. Yes, it was enough.*

17

Of course it's enough to love somebody, of course you did enough. All night long, all day Saturday and Sunday, those words played in my head. And come Monday morning, the words were still there. On the way to school, while I was in school, it's all I could think about. She did enough. Monnie did so much.

But I wanted more.

I wanted her to stay with me.

Still . . . well, I still had one more big job to do, one more family to look over. Yet looking was just tearing my heart out.

I had a thought then—I could ask Jane to come looking with me. Why not? We could do it today in town. No, it wasn't night, and it wasn't dark. But I could walk by, see how things were with the Alley people. And it would sure save me from a long walk in the dark to town some night. And having Jane along—well, maybe it could help.

As soon as the recess bell rang, I grabbed Jane and pulled her over to the side of the schoolyard by the fence.

"After school today," I said. "What are you doing?"

But instead of answering, she said, "Guess what? I saw Johnny and Buck and my pa yesterday. And guess what?"

"What?" I said. "Tell me!"

"Buck is fine, and so is Johnny, but they're so sad, they really want to come home. And Miss Cotter, she actually said that in a month or so—by May—we could!"

"Really? Home?"

"Really." She grinned at me.

"And your pa?" I said.

"He's sort of okay," she answered, but she was frowning. "He's all cleaned up and shaved. And sober." She took a deep breath. "He seems awful sad, though."

"'Cause he misses you."

She nodded. "He does. He said he did. And he has big plans for when we get together again. He said he's going to build a new room on the house so I can have my own room and not have to share with Buck

138

and Johnny. And when we get back home, back on the mountain, then you and me, we can play again and I can see you and everything." She made a face. "And I won't miss Reverend Hornby one little bit."

"So what are you doing today?" I asked. "Right now. After school."

She frowned. "What day is it? Monday? Bible lessons. But not till tonight. Why?"

"Can you get out this afternoon?" I said.

She shook her head no. "Not to play. Never. They never let me do that."

"Not to play," I said. "Go home and make up an excuse. Say you have to come back to school. Say— I don't know—say Miss Ford wants you to stay after for something."

"Stay after?" she said. "I'd get killed!"

"Not stay after, like punishment!" I said. I thought quickly. "Bulletin board. Miss Ford wants help putting up a spring bulletin board."

"She does?" Jane said.

I sighed. "No, silly. She doesn't. I just meant you can use that as an excuse."

"For what?"

I hesitated. I hadn't told her about spying. Hadn't told her about my worry about who would take care of me. She might have thought about it. But neither of us had said a word.

"I have to spy on someone," I said.

She made a face at me. *"Spy?"*

"Yes, spy." And then, I took a deep breath. "You know about Monnie?" I said. "How sick she is?"

She nodded

I looked down at the ground. "Well, I need a place to live," I said. "If she dies."

"She's not going to die," Jane said.

"She says she is. And I have no place to go. No one to live with."

"Oh, if only my ma was alive!" she said. "Ma would take you in with us in a second. She'd take good care of you, too."

I nodded. "I know," I said. For just a minute, I felt tears well up. "But I need a home, and Monnie and me, we've talked to some folks about taking me in."

And then I told her about the spying part, about looking in on the Boltons and the Cravens. And about the Alley people.

"Poor Monnie," Jane whispered. And then she put out a hand and touched mine, just a little brush of her fingers. "Poor you," she said.

"I'm okay," I said. "But will you come with me this afternoon?"

She took a deep breath. "Yes!" she said. "I'll probably get killed, but I'm going to do it. I'm not even going to ask. I'm just going to be late coming home.

If they don't like it—too bad."

That's how come, when school was over, Jane and I were walking through town, across the railroad tracks, headed for where the Alley folks lived.

We were laughing as we walked, both of us so happy we were almost silly. It had been so long since we'd had an afternoon to play, to be together.

"Isn't town a strange place?" Jane asked as we walked. "Too many folks and too many lights, and just plain too many things. I can't wait till I go back up mountain."

I nodded. "It's different," I said. "The people are different. Really different."

We stepped over a huge, reddish dog that was sleeping in a patch of sun, stretched out right in the middle of the sidewalk by the hardware store.

"Hi, dog!" Jane said. She bent down and patted him, and I squatted alongside her. His head was hot from the sun, and I could feel lumpy places around his ears—probably fleas.

The dog didn't move, just looked up, flapped its tail a few times, then closed its eyes again.

I stood up. "Even the dogs are different," I said. "Up home, that dog'd be barking its head off at us. That's a dog's job."

Jane slid her eyes sideways at me. "Could you live in town?"

I shrugged. "Don't know. Have to see."

We started walking again, coming to a small triangle of green where two alleys connect behind some houses. The alley doesn't have a name, not that I've ever heard, anyway. And the house that sits there has always just been called the Alley house. The people who live in it are called the Alley people. Everyone knows they have names—Alice and Nathan—but that's how it is sometimes. Things and people get a name for themselves, and it sticks.

Jane looked at me as we turned down the alley. "You really think you could live here?"

I shrugged. "I told you I don't know. I've got to live someplace. And Monnie says they're possibles. They've been coming up mountain for ages. You know that. You know they've got cousins and kissing cousins up home."

"I know," Jane said. "But they're awful strange."

I nodded. They are strange. But they're not crazy, even though some say they are. Only thing is—they talk to animals. Well, lots of people do, I know. But these two, they say animals answer them back. And they actually understand what the animals say to them. They can tell you every single thing a horse is thinking, or a cat or a dog. And when you watch the horse or dog or cat, it seems real sensible, like that is exactly what the creature is thinking. The Alley people even say they can understand the frogs. And their house is so crowded with creatures, well—you wonder, where could a human fit?

Still, I had promised myself I would look them over, and as we came around the corner, there they were. Both Nathan and Alice were sitting on their porch, a couple of dogs at their feet, cats sleeping in groups or twining themselves around everywhere. A whole line of birdcages was strung up along the edge of the porch, but the cage doors were open, and birds were flitting this way and that. There was even one bird perched on a cat's head. The cat either didn't notice, or didn't care, because it was fast asleep. Nathan was wearing a thick, fur hat, like you wear in the winter, though it was really warm that afternoon. He had his nose in a book, and his sister, Alice, had cards spread out on a table in front of her. She was stuffing herself with something, pork rinds it looked like. Alice is always stuffing herself with something. She's bulky and squatty, like something you'd see sitting on a lily pad. Funny thing is, I don't think she'd be insulted if you told her that. The window was open slightly behind them, and I could hear music playing, soft and soothing, coming from the radio somewhere inside the house.

As we came up the walk, they both looked up and smiled at us. "Afternoon," Nathan called, lifting one hand in a wave.

"Hi," Jane said.

"Afternoon," I said. It sounded kind of formal, but that's the way Monnie taught me—to greet folks the way they greet you.

He marked his place in his book with his finger. "Come to visit with us?" he said.

"No," I said. "Just came to . . . to . . ."

To spy on you.

I felt my face getting hot.

"We're just on our way home," Jane said. Though how we could be on the way home and passing by here, I didn't know.

Alice bent and lifted a cat that was twining itself around her ankles. She snuggled it to her face. "This here's Archibald," she called out. "He says he's happy you stopped by. Come set and talk to us a bit."

I looked at Jane.

She shook her head just slightly. Neither of us really wanted to stop.

"Jane has to get home," I said. And that was surely the truth.

"Well, a cookie couldn't hold you up long, could it now?" Nathan said. "I be right back." He stood up and smiled at us before turning to go into the house.

And that's when his hat flew off. No. No, it did not fly off. His hat jumped off! It landed on its feet, all four feet, and then scurried to a corner of the porch and disappeared. It was a huge, fat, black skunk. I saw it just long enough to know for sure.

In just a moment, Nathan was back with a plate of cookies. "Help yourself, take a whole lot," he said, coming to the edge of the porch, and holding the plate out to Jane and me.

I took just one, keeping my head bent, feeling awkward and flustery inside. Did they know I was looking them over? Monnie said she had talked to folks about having me. So they must have known. And . . . were they right this minute looking me over?

"Take more'n one!" Nathan said. "Made them myself."

"Oh, will you listen to that man!" Alice said, her voice stern, but I could tell she was teasing. "He is just full of baloney. He couldn't make himself a bite to eat if his life depended on it."

"I made me a baloney sandwich once," Nathan said quietly.

Jane and I both laughed. I took another cookie. They were really wonderful—lemon with something crunchy and sweet on top.

I looked up.

Nathan was still holding out the plate and smiling at me.

I've heard it said that if Nathan weren't an old man, he'd have every woman in the county after him with that smile. Folks say that saints smile like that. The only saints I've ever seen are the pictures on those holy cards at the funeral parlor, and those saints all look like they're about to puke but are holding it back. But Nathan's smile, that's something to see.

He put the plate down on the railing, then went back and sat down. Right away, two cats landed in his lap, and he set about making room for them both.

Alice was still cuddling Archibald, but with one hand, she beckoned to me. "Bring that there plate," she said, pointing to the cookie plate.

I brought it over and set it on the table by her.

"Thank you kindly," she said. "Stop by and visit some more when you have time." She suddenly reached up, grabbed my hand, and pulled me close.

I felt my heart thumping wildly. She was going to say something about Monnie, about living here. But all she did was stuff a handful of cookies in my pocket.

And then she did the same to Jane.

"There!" she said. "That should hold you for the walk home."

We both thanked her, and then Jane and I turned to go.

As we went down the steps, I was thinking—they were sweet, really sweet. And I'd like the animals, too—at least, I think I would. Only thing was—they lived in town. And I didn't know how I could leave Star Mountain. And yet—I had to live someplace.

At the edge of the yard, Jane and I turned and waved.

Alice still had Archibald in her arms, and she made him lift one paw, like he was waving good-bye.

"Come back and see us, you hear?" Alice called.

"We will!" Jane called back, waving again. "We'll be back."

I waved, too.

But I didn't say anything.

18

Funny how things go out of your life. Like music. We'd had no music for so long—excepting that dreadful Easter service—that when suddenly it was back, it scared me almost. It was late in the day, already almost dark, when I neared our door—and heard music coming from inside. Music. Soft, beautiful music.

At first, I thought: an angel's song! It was an angel, come to escort Monnie away. I knew it was foolish to think that way. I stopped on the porch, not able to step inside, nor even turn the knob. But after a minute, it was clear who made that music, and it wasn't any angel. Somehow, Monnie had found the strength to pick up the fiddle and bow.

Carefully, I opened the door. There was Monnie, sitting in the chair by the front window, a quilt over her lap, her fiddle tucked under her chin, one foot wiggling like she wanted to go on and tap it—just like old times. She was playing something sweet and melancholy enough to melt a person's soul.

Her eyes met mine, and they smiled, and she bent over that fiddle again, putting such sound into it, such sweetness. I just sat down on the floor, slid off my shoes, and eased myself into listening.

She finished that song and began a different one, "Sweet By and By," my favorite, her favorite, my mama's favorite. The way she played it now, it was sweet, yet so lonesome it almost broke my heart. When she finished, she laid the bow in her lap, then laid the fiddle alongside it. She took a deep, sweet, easy breath then, and we smiled at one another.

"Been a while," Monnie said. "Hardly knowed if I could do it."

I just nodded.

Monnie's breath began coming short and fast then, like she'd been running, and her lips got kind of white. But there was still a smile on her face, an ease that hadn't been there in a while.

After her breath began to come easier, I asked, "Can you play another?"

She just shook her head.

I nodded. Okay. But, I told myself, if music could come back to our lives, who could say what else might come back? Maybe Monnie herself could come back to me, the old Monnie, the way she used to be. Maybe God was going to grant me my miracle.

That whole night, Monnie seemed better, even ate a bit of beans and pork. And so, next day, I hurried home, hoping for more. Hoping she'd keep being better.

And sure enough, when I got there she was playing again, the music loud enough to hear right through the walls. This time, there was no need to stop by the door, fearful-like, because I knew what was inside. And it wouldn't be an angel!

I went in softly, so as not to disturb the music. And I sat down, and nodded at Monnie, and settled myself to listen.

Monnie was better, she had to be! I listened as she so gently, so quietly, played those songs. There was none of her old liveliness in the music, none of her toe-tapping stuff. But there was plenty of heart, so much it felt as though that fiddle was talking straight from her heart to mine.

First "Uncloudy Day," and then "Dear Companion," and then—then, she played "Amazing Grace." Oh, how that song makes my heart ache. And always, always, it makes me cry. I don't think it makes me sad. It's as though it reaches inside me, turns a little key inside my heart, something that loosens up the tears and lets them out. I guess when a heart gets touched that way, that's what happens. Leastwise, that's the way it happens to me.

I let the tears pour right down my face, not even trying to stop them.

After that was done, Monnie rested, laying the fiddle across her lap, her breath so raspy and wicked that I watched her hard for a while. I could feel my own heart beating hard for her, my own breathing coming fast.

It took a while for her breathing to get even sort of near normal, but after a while, she began to breathe better, and color came back to her lips.

She laid her head back in her chair then. "Tell you what, girl," she said softly. "I believe there'll be music where I'm going."

Don't talk that way. Please don't talk that way, Monnie. But I didn't say that out loud.

"And beans and grits," she continued, a little smile playing round her lips. "I think there'll be beans and grits there, too. Can't imagine a God that wouldn't have beans and grits, can you?"

She lifted her head from the back of the chair and looked at me.

"Guess not," I said. But the words came out kind of strangled sounding. I tried to keep looking at her, to let her know it was all right to talk. But my heart was thundering away inside me. And I kept my hands folded tightly in my lap.

She laid her head back again. "And know what else, girl?"

"What?" I said.

"Well," she said. "I'm looking forward to seeing my man. Saw him one night, you know. Your grampa. He comed right here to my room. He's waiting for me. Said when the time comed, he'd be here to take my hand."

I gulped, a sobbing sound I didn't mean to make. It just burst out of me. I tried to cover it with a laugh. "He came to your room?" I asked.

Monnie nodded. "It ain't so strange. Who says folks can't come back when you need them?"

Tears rushed up my throat, and with them came words, words and tears, all mixed up together, all spilling out together. "What about me?" I said.

"What you mean?"

I swallowed hard. "Will you come back to me? If I need you?" I asked.

She lifted her head again, smiling at me a little. "Why, 'course I will. If the good Lord lets me. Don't know what the rules be there."

She was quiet a while, and I didn't say anything more, either. It took all my strength just not to cry out loud.

"It'll be all right," Monnie said after a while. "Don't you fret. I know you. Known you for eleven whole years. You going to do just fine. You wait and see."

I didn't answer. What could I say? Again, I wanted to tell her to stop. But time was short now, I could tell, and I didn't want to regret anything, not a single thing. Still, I could hardly bear to listen.

"Just one more thing," Monnie said. "Just one. Last thing for today."

Like she had heard my thoughts.

"It's okay," I said. "What?"

"They're digging me a grave," she said. "Now, don't fret yourself. It's got to be done. Saw them out of the window today. It'll be ready when I'm ready."

I swallowed. "A grave?"

She nodded. "A grave. Got a coffin box, too. Ogden Zuckerman's making it. He used the sides of a old wagon, told me hisself." She laughed then. "Told him, maybe he should just bury me in the wagon. That way, it could carry me right on to heaven."

"Oh," I said. Because—what else could a person say?

I got up then, went to the window, and looked out.

Far off, far toward the angle between the yard and

the beginning of the creek bed, I saw it. It's where the old graves are—Monnie's other babies that died before they saw the light of day, my grampa's grave, my mama's and papa's graves. I couldn't see the hole from here. But I could see the pile of dirt dug from that hole.

A grave. A hole. A grave for Monnie.

I turned back from the window, then turned to Monnie. I knew I was supposed to say something. But what? But Monnie's eyes were closed, and she looked so peaceful. She was even snoring a bit, like she'd worn herself down with the music. And with talk. For the moment, even her breath was coming easy.

Let her rest.

I went to the door then, walked myself out to that hole in the ground. I stood over it, looking down.

A hole. A grave. For when Monnie's dead, gone and left me. Left all of us, left the whole wide world of us. I looked up and around me, as if I could puzzle it out.

It had already begun to grow dark, and a couple of snowflakes wandered down, lazy-like, as if they didn't really mean to amount to anything.

I watched as night creatures came out, saw a fox hightailing it across the top of the ridge. A herd of deer appeared on the ridge, too, followed by a coyote, all by its lonesome. An owl screeched some-where and then was still. Suddenly, something flew close to my face, so close I could feel the beat of its wings, something fast, like an owl. Then there was the death scream of a small creature, caught up in that owl's claws. I prayed that it wasn't a rabbit.

I stood for a long, long time, heard more sounds—a coyote calling, another answering back—*eeih, eeih,* like a child crying. And then all was still again.

I stood there for just another minute, thinking, wondering, trying to figure this place without Monnie. What would the night be like, I wondered? What about snowflakes, and deer and bears and owls? Would they all be the same?

No. They wouldn't be the same. Nothing would be the same. It would all be different.

It would be so very different. And I didn't know how I'd manage.

I just shook my head. And then I turned to go back in. But before I stepped up on the porch, I whispered a prayer to God. Not a prayer for a mira-cle. Nothing like that. Not anymore. I think I just called His name.

And then I went on into the house.

19

I kept thinking Monnie couldn't get any sicker, that it was get better or die. Still, neither happened. She just got weaker and weaker. She lay in her bed most days, only coming out of her room for supper—not that she ate anything. But she did sit with me, pretending to eat. I'd beg her and beg her, and finally, she'd take a sip or two of soup, but not enough to keep a chipmunk alive. And then, when she did take a sip, her hand shook so bad she could hardly bring the spoon to her mouth.

And there was no more music. It was as if those two days had been sort of a last fling, just something to remind us both that there was still music left somewhere. Or maybe it was Monnie's way of telling herself there'd be music where she was going.

It got so I didn't want to go home after school. I knew there was so little time left. I knew I should spend every moment with her. Yet I couldn't. It just hurt so much looking at her that way, thin and frail, listening to her wicked, raspy breathing. And once she got room for the breath to go in, then she couldn't get it out again, and she'd gag over that stuck breath.

So most days, I didn't get home till dark, supper time almost, when I'd eat and tuck up Monnie in bed. And then, one day, I found myself in town, lurking around the doorway of the clinic again, thinking about Dr. Harkins. I had a secret worry, and I couldn't think of who else to talk to, who else to turn to. I had Jane, but I felt like I needed a grown-up for this one. Monnie trusted him, even if he was town folks. And if she did, then I knew I could, too. Not only that, but I think I just plain needed someone to talk to. I was getting awful lonesome.

So that's how come I found myself sitting in that chair by his desk one afternoon after school.

"How you getting on, Blessing?" he asked when I sat down. "How's Monnie? Any different?"

"She's worse," I said.

"I could come up and see her."

I shook my head. "She doesn't want anyone. She's getting ready to die."

He raised his eyebrows at me.

I nodded. "She's talking about stuff," I said. "You know, about graves and coffins and about music and things like . . . like me." I took a deep breath and looked away.

"What about you?" he said.

I wanted to tell him, tell him about me looking for a place to live—people to live with. I wanted to tell him my worry. It's why I had come here. But I didn't know. . . .

"I don't tell secrets, you know," he said, like he was mind reading.

"I know that," I said.

"I really don't," he said.

I looked at him. "What about to Miss Cotter?" I said.

He frowned. "Why should I tell her? What you tell me stays here. Right with us. I don't tell anyone."

"Never?" I said.

He smiled and put his hand over his heart. "Never. Promise."

"Well," I said, and I took a deep breath. "I need a home. Someone to live with."

"I know," he said quietly, like he had thought of that himself.

"Yes," I said. "And—and well, Monnie and me, we have some places picked out."

"*Some* places?" he said.

I nodded. "Some. We're not decided on one just yet. Soon, though."

"That's good," he said.

"Uh-huh." I took another deep breath. "So, what I want to know is—if I go there—wherever it is I decide to go—can anybody take me away? Like they did with Jane?"

Because that was my worry. I needed to know that I'd be safe, that nobody would come and snatch me away. If I had to have another home, I had to know that I wouldn't get pulled out of it, sent to someone mean like had happened with Jane.

"*Jane?*" he asked.

"Yes," I said, impatient. "You know, Jane, my friend, Jane Collier. They took her away from her papa. And sent her to the minister."

"Oh," he said. "That's different. No. Of course they won't take you away. Monnie can appoint guardians for you. If the guardians accept." He looked at me. "Did they?"

I nodded. "But I know we need pieces of paper, formal-like, right?"

"Yes. But knowing Monnie, she has it all done up correctly."

"She has," I said. "She already told me. She has one made out for each place. I choose, and it will be all laid out clear on that piece of paper. But once she's . . . you know . . . gone, that's what I'm worried about. So nobody can snatch me away and make me live where I don't want to live? You sure?"

"'Course I'm sure. Nobody is going to do that to you. Monnie wouldn't let you go to places that aren't good for you. Nobody will take you away."

"How do you know?"

"I know," he said. "I give you my word. If they try, I'll take care of it."

I sucked in a deep breath, relieved. "That's okay, then," I said. And I stood up to go.

"You sure that's all?" he said.

"That's all," I said. "I'll go home now."

"Want company?" he said. "I have no more patients today. I can leave now. We can walk together to the end of town."

I looked at him, surprised. I'd never seen him outside the clinic. Well, in the post office once or at the bank when I was with Monnie. But it seemed that he belonged here in this building, lived here. I shrugged. "Okay," I said. "If you want."

He smiled at me, then got his pipe and his jacket, and we went down the hall. In the waiting room, Miss Cotter turned to look at us, but I pretended not to see her. And nosy Miss Dorris, the nurse, she almost fell out of her chair. I knew she'd be dying to know what we were talking about and where we were going.

"Know what?" Dr. Harkins said as we turned the corner and headed away from town. "I heard spring frogs today."

"They been on the mountain for weeks," I said.

"Probably been around here, too," he said. "But we don't hear them the way you do up mountain."

I just shook my head. I couldn't imagine living in town. And that made me think of the Alley people. Nathan and Alice, they were nice. They were really, really nice. But town? No.

"You don't much like town, do you?" Dr. Harkins said.

"Not much," I said.

"You're like your grandma that way."

I nodded. "I guess."

"Skunk cabbages are up in the woods, too," he went on. "Saw some pushing their way up. Right through the snow."

"They stink," I said.

He nodded. "Yup."

We went on a while then, side by side, not saying much. I was walking fast, the way I always do when I'm in town. Once we got to the edge of town, though, I slowed down. When we reached the winding road that led to the mountain, we were strolling, real leisurely-like.

"You can go now," I said.

"It's all right," he said. "I'll walk awhile with you. If you don't mind."

"Suit yourself," I said.

We turned and started up mountain then. It was harder walking, leaning into the slope of the hill, so neither of us said much. Yet it felt all right to be quiet like that. I noticed, though, that the whole time we walked, he was looking at his feet, frowning down at them. I wondered if he was thinking he might crunch one of those frogs if he didn't watch his step. Never can tell what town folks think when they're set loose in the out-of-doors.

But I guess I was wrong about his thinking, because after a while, he looked over at me and said quietly, "Blessing, you're about fit to bust, aren't you?"

I looked at him. "Bust?" I said. "No."

"No?"

"'Course not," I said.

We had to make a little detour then, stepping over a tiny brook that had suddenly appeared with the thawing of the snows. I slid a look at him, wondering what he was getting at. Though I thought maybe I knew.

"I guess," he said, "what I'm thinking is this. If it

were me, I'd want to cry. And scream. Maybe even hit things. And if I had nobody much to talk to—then I'd feel fit to bust."

I just shook my head. I didn't feel fit to bust. Just—like crying sometimes. But I didn't say that, didn't say anything.

He was quiet a bit, and then he said, "And I guess I'd be hurting something awful."

I shivered then, as the sun slipped lower, felt the cold of the mountain shadow on my back. I stepped to the side of the path where there was still a bit of sunlight. "Yes," I said. "Sometimes it hurts." I sighed. "Sometimes it hurts real bad."

He took my hand then. Just reached out and took it. He seemed kind of shy when he did it, and his eyebrows went up, like he was asking, Is this okay? I nodded.

We stood for just a moment, hand in hand like that. His hand felt soft, almost like a girl's hand, and I realized I had probably never held a man's hand before. But it was okay. And truth to tell—it even felt sort of good.

Suddenly it was almost dark, night just dropping down so quick, the way it does on the mountain, the shadows stretching long and blue. I pulled my hand out of his gently, not wanting to hurt his feelings. "You'd best get back," I said. "And hurry or you won't find your way in the dark."

"Can you find your way?" he asked.

I laughed, couldn't help it. "Like I've not been born on this mountainside!" I said.

He smiled, too. "Come back and talk to me again?" he said.

I nodded.

For a moment, he just stood and looked at me. And then he turned and left.

I watched him go, watched the shadow of the mountain across his back, watched how the sun, with a last fling of rays, lit up his hair.

He turned back to me then, as though he knew I was watching. And then he lifted a hand.

I waved back, and turned and climbed into the dark. I thought of all those times on the mountain with Monnie, all the times we walked fast against the setting of this same sun. I thought of the times we'd work in the garden, trying to get it planted before the sun was gone, building up the fences and rails to keep out the pesky rabbits and deer. In my mind, I could see the setting sun streaking across Monnie's big shoulders, her hair in wisps around her face, streaks of dirt and sweat across her forehead. And I remembered the times after those hot days, when we'd worked hard and we'd treat ourselves to a trip to Ellie's cabin.

I walked on faster then, racing the moon that was already creeping over the mountaintop, racing the shadows that stretched out into the night. One star peeped out at me, shining pale in the blue-black sky. All about me were the sounds of the mountain calling to me, calling me home—the wind soughing in the trees, the spring peepers shouting their mating calls. And a coyote crying out his lonesome mountain song.

20

Mountain people, when they see a need, they do something about it. Now, for instance, folks were caring for Monnie and me. We never asked. We never ever saw a soul. Still, every day, things appeared at our door. I'd open the door in the morning or the evening, and there'd be a big pot of soup, or a pork-and-bean casserole, or a plate full of rice and beans or barbecue. Sometimes I'd find a pot full of squirrel stew, bones and all, with the meat still sticking to them. Or there'd be corn bread and apple butter.

Some folks, the ones who didn't have much of their own, still they left what they could. One morning, I found sunflower seeds, dried up from last year's gardens, and an old seed catalogue for Monnie to look through. Another morning, there was a chunk of dried venison. People knew that bad times had come to us, and they were doing the best they could to help us through. It did help, too, 'cause I wasn't much of a cook.

After supper, I'd wash out the pot real good and leave it on the step, sometimes with a gift of my own inside—a pretty leaf or a few wooden beads, or whatever I had to spare. In the morning, it'd be gone, and something else would've taken its place.

This night, when I got home from walking with Dr. Harkins, there was a pot on the porch by the door, and I lifted it, sniffing deeply. Beans. Beans with pork and tomatoes and lots of onions. Just the smell made me hungry.

I went on inside, put the pot on the stove. The lamps hadn't been lit yet, but a light was on in Monnie's room by her bed. I tiptoed in, fearful like I always was. Was she still—there? Still breathing?

"Monnie?" I said.

She leaned a hand out at me, and she sighed.

I went to the bed and took her hand. "We got beans and onions and tomatoes," I said. "A whole big pot of it."

She smiled. "Sounds like Sally Martin's doings. It's about all she can cook."

"I'll set the table," I said.

She shook her head. "Just set a while?" she said. She patted the bed beside her.

I sat down, but not on the bed, because I didn't want to jiggle her and make her start coughing. Instead, I pulled the chair over from the window and put it beside her bed.

"I been thinking something," Monnie said.

"What?" I said.

"Thinking maybe you'd stay by me here tonight," she said.

I felt my heart begin thudding hard. "Okay," I said.

But why, why? Are you going? Are you dying? Please don't go.

"That be all right with you?" Monnie said. She turned her face to me. She was smiling, but I thought I saw loneliness in her eyes. Or fear.

"Sure it's all right," I said, trying to make my voice cheerful.

"You go get yourself a bite," she said. "Then come on back."

"You're not getting up?" I said.

She shook her head.

"Shall I bring your supper here?"

"No, don't want nothing," she said. She looked at me a moment. "Maybe later," she said softly.

And how come I knew—knew she said that just to make me feel better? That she wasn't planning on eating, not at all.

"I'll be back," I said.

I hurried to the kitchen, made myself a plate of the beans and tomatoes, then carried it back to her room. I sat on the floor, using the chair seat as my table, and began to eat. It should have tasted wonderful; it smelled wonderful. But I had no stomach for it, not for anything. Each bite was harder to swallow than the one before. And after a bit, I pushed it aside, then laid my head against Monnie's bed.

She reached out a hand and touched my hair. "You got pretty hair," she said. "You got your mama's hair."

I had heard that before, and I just smiled.

We were quiet a bit. And then she said, "Where you think you'll go?"

I didn't have to ask what she meant. I knew. I swallowed. "I'm thinking the Boltons," I said.

"That's good," she said. "That's real, real good. They'll treat you fine. That paper is all signed up and in the bank."

I blinked hard. "Too many Cravens," I said.

"Lord, yes," she said. "I figured as much."

"And I couldn't live in town," I said. I could hardly speak, had to keep swallowing.

"That'd be hard," Monnie said. "But now, don't forget them papers. They's all made out in the bank. One for each family. Dr. Harkins can help you sort them out if you need help. I told Poppy I thought you might come to them."

"Oh, Monnie!" I said.

"I know," she said. "I know." And she patted my hair again, and again whispered, "I know." She kept on patting my hair, stroking my head.

But she couldn't know. Nobody knew.

For a long time, we sat there quietly. I was fighting tears, forcing them down. I didn't want to cry, didn't want to make her even sadder. But my heart was just breaking. Outside the windows, it became dark, fully dark, and the moon crept in and lay across the foot of her bed. In the woods, an owl called and was answered by another, and I heard the branch scraping against my window, that familiar sound I've known my whole life. I don't know how long we stayed like that, Monnie just stroking my hair. But it must have been a long time, maybe a very long time. And then—then, I must have slept. Because suddenly I was awakened, awakened because she was speaking, her voice stronger than in a long time.

"Girl!" she said to me. "Hear that, girl?"

I lifted my head. "What, Monnie?" I asked. "What? The owl?"

"No!" she said. "No. That—the music. You hear that music?"

I listened, but I didn't hear any music. I heard only her raggedy breath and the branch scraping the windowpane. But Monnie's head was tipped to one side, and I knew she was hearing something else, something different.

She took my hand then, lying there on her cover, and she held it tight, tight with more strength than I ever thought she had.

"Girl," she whispered, lifting my hand to her face, and pressing it to her cheek. "Girl, I been humming along in the key of C for a long time now. Long time. I've just switched to B." She tilted her head, seemed to listen some more. "B flat, I think."

She sighed, then laid my hand gently back on the cover.

"Monnie!" I said. I stood up and leaned over her. "Monnie!"

She breathed softly. "It's time now," she said.

I wanted to think she was wandering in her head, talking about long-gone music, talking nonsense. But I knew better. She wasn't wandering in her head, she wasn't.

But it couldn't be time. Couldn't be.

"Not yet, Monnie," I whispered to her. "Don't go yet."

"Girl," she said. "I just switched keys. That's all. You 'member that, you hear?"

I wanted to answer, wanted to say yes, yes, say anything at all, anything she wanted me to say, anything to keep her here. But I couldn't. I couldn't say a word. Tears were welling up, sudden and fast, fierce, spilling over because I knew—knew as well as she did, that something had come into this room. Something we'd been expecting for too long.

"Monnie?" I said.

She didn't answer for a bit. And then she said, "It's sweet what God gived to me. Sweet."

"What, Monnie?" I said. "What's sweet? What did God give? Tell me. Talk to me."

Because if she kept talking, if I kept her talking, she couldn't die—right?

She sighed a little. "Why, you, girl," she whispered.

She sighed then, in and out, in and out, the softest breaths I'd heard in so long, no gasping or struggling at all.

I took long, sweet breaths with her, easy breaths, so happy. She was breathing easy, she was! And maybe, maybe we had it all wrong, maybe there was time yet.

Together we breathed, in and out, in and out. I rested my head beside her own.

And then she was breathing no more.

Monnie? Monnie?

I bent over, looked in her face.

"Monnie?" I whispered, taking her hand. "Monnie, don't go!"

But there was no keeping her here, no tugging her back from where she'd gone. And she was gone, already gone, gone away, gone somewhere, to her man, her music, the far side of the mountain, maybe.

Gone to God.

21

Tears were running down my cheeks, dripping off my chin and nose, and I didn't even try to stop them. No need to hide them anymore. No need. Monnie was gone. Gone.

I got up and went to the window then, struggled to open it, but I was crying so hard that I couldn't see the latch, my tears dropping right down onto the windowsill. I wiped my face on my sleeve, found the latch, turned it and threw the window open—wide, wide. Wide, so that Monnie's soul could come and go in the night.

"It's open now," I whispered to her. "You can come and go. You can come in. The window's open."

I was crying the whole time, wiping away tears that wouldn't stop. I rubbed my sleeve across my nose and looked out the window, thinking about what Monnie had told me. It's an old mountain tale, but maybe it's true. Monnie said you got to leave a window open the first days after a person dies so the soul can come and go. That's because it's hard for a soul at first, let loose from its body after a whole lifetime of sticking together. It feels scared, like a child the first time away from its mama. So it needs a bit of security, needs to come back to its body once in a while for the first day or two. Or at least till it gets the hang of being on its own once and for all. I didn't know if Monnie believed it or not. I didn't know if I believed it. But just in case, I wanted the window open, didn't want her wandering scared. Wanted her to have a place to come home to.

It was cold in the room then, and I went and got a quilt from the chest. I wrapped myself in it, shivering. I sat myself near the window, in the chair that the moon sits in. I closed my eyes, made pictures behind my eyelids: pictures of Monnie floating on the wind, in and out of that window, over to the graveyard. I could see her standing with her man, see her with my mama, see her cradling a child to herself, two children, one in each arm, those babies that were buried out in the graveyard long ago. Her breathing was sweet, easy and sweet, no more strangled, choking kinds of breath. I made her look different, too, in my imaginings—tall and strong again, not all shrunken up like she'd gotten to be. I made her head big like a lion's on her big strong neck, just the way it used to be, her breasts full and round now, ready to feed those babies.

She had to be feeling better now, had to be, with her babies and her man, and able to breathe again. But what about me, what about me? I missed her. I missed her already. Oh, Lord, I did.

Tears were running out of my eyes, even though I kept them shut tight. What would I do without her?

And what about music—was there music where she was—and beans and grits, like she once said? Must be, must be all good things out there in God's land where she was now.

Only thing missing was me. She'd want to talk to me. She would, I knew she would. I sat up straight, opened my eyes and looked all around me, slow and careful. She told me that she'd come back if I needed her—if the Lord let her. Maybe right now she would? Didn't I need her now? I did.

But no. There was no Monnie coming out of the corners, no shadows, just my own imaginings to keep me company. And Monnie lying dead in her bed over there.

I sat back shivering, huddled my blanket closer. All night, I sat there wakeful, nursing my imaginings, sat while the stars dimmed, winked off one by one, till a faint streak of light showed itself across the east.

I got up then and left the room. I didn't even look down at Monnie, couldn't bear to. Not just yet.

I went out to the porch and stood looking at the mountain. Soft morning light touched the sides of the peaks, and mist crept over the ground. Mourning doves were *coo, cooing,* sounding extra sad this morning. I saw deer, a whole herd of them. They crept from the woods, down into the meadow, quiet as the morning light. They found their eating place and bent to it. But one of them, the one set guard to watch, an old one with scruffy fur on her rump, she turned to me, looking troubled. She stayed that way a long time while the others went on to eat.

A fox came slinking along the ridge, his tail down, a sorry-looking sight, as if his heart wasn't into being a fox any longer. And then, he suddenly veered and headed down to the meadow. The deer just watched him, as if he made no matter to them at all. And then, it seemed that fox came to pay its respects. It trotted right up near the house, stood and looked at me. It was so close, I could see the lashes round its eyes, the whiskers on its mouth tremble with its breath. It stood there sniffing, then bent its head deep before it turned and hightailed it back to the ridge.

A groundhog showed himself, practically at my feet, setting up on his haunches, his little brown head turning this way and that, sniffing the air, his paws together like in prayer.

And then I saw someone slipping through the mist. Ellie, it was Ellie, and she was bringing me a gift—food. She carried it in two hands, a heavy pot from the look of it.

She stepped up on the porch, and I took the pot from her. "She's gone," I whispered. "Monnie is gone."

Her face got all crumpled up looking and she put out a hand to me. She patted my shoulder, her hand heavy, awkward. "I'll be back," she whispered. "Right back."

And then she slipped away into the mist.

It was light enough now to see by, and I went back in the house. I put the iron kettle on to boil. I had a job to do, and I'd do it. No one else would touch her.

When the water was hot, I poured it into a basin, put the soap in, and swirled it round. I didn't use the harsh stuff, that lye soap, but the fatty, smooth soap that Monnie made for baths. I took the whole thing, basin, towels, and soap into Monnie's room. I bathed her then, washed her face, her hands, her whole entire body, even her feet. I washed her hair, too. It was hard to do, but I did it.

There was no need to press her eyes closed because they were already closed, and they stayed that way. She was seeing things now, things only dead people see. Then I changed her nightdress. She weighed no more than one of the feathers that floats out of the sky on a summer's day. When I had her clean and prettied up, I pulled up the blanket. I'd need help to change the bed, to wrap her in clean sheets. But someone would be by. And then we'd lay her out and bury her.

For some reason, my tears had stopped, like maybe I was cried out. For now, anyway.

I went to the window and leaned my elbows on the sill.

And then, like spirits out of the mists, I saw them. Mountain people. Neighbors.

As the sun rose over the mountain, they came to me. First came the Boltons, Mason and Poppy and old Georgie, who was carrying Child. Behind them were the Cravens, but thank the Lord, I didn't see any of their children. Behind them was Ellie. I knew she would help me with Monnie. I breathed easier because I wanted that bed clean, Monnie fixed up good for her trip home.

I went and opened the door and they came in, knowing they were welcome. Ellie must have spread the word, because dozens of folks came behind them, some I'd not seen in a year, and some I saw most every week. Reverend Tucker came, and he didn't say a word, he took my hand, which was just right. Some folks came inside; some stayed out on the porch, liking it better that way.

They brought flowers: forsythia, yellow and full bloomed, and daffodils, not opened yet, with bits of yellow peeping through their folded green skins. They brought tobacco and spirits and food, so much food. Soon the house felt warmed and good.

After a while, Ellie took me by the hand, and we went to Monnie's room. Ellie bent over the bed, then stood up, and looked at me. "Why, Miss Blessing," she said. "You done it all. Done her up good. The Lord'll be pleased to see her that way."

"I need help, though," I said. "The linens need changing."

Ellie nodded, and she set to doing things. She showed me other things to do, too, things one should do for a body that's dead. After that was done, there was nothing else to do.

Folks came in then, womenfolks mostly, and they took turns sitting by Monnie, staying awake while she slept. Each of them said something to me. But even though I heard, and said thank you, I have no idea what was said.

After a while, I felt tired, and went out onto the porch to sit. That's when Poppy came and stood by me.

He was quiet for a long time. And then he spoke softly. "We got you a room," he said. "Fixed up nice."

I stared up at him.

"When you ready," he said. "You stay here long as you want. We're wanting you when you're wanting to come." He tugged at his beard then, and shifted some, like he wanted to get away. I realized—I'd never in my whole entire life heard him say that many words at one time.

I tried to think what to say to him. Something, something. But no words came out. My heart was thumping hard. A room. Of course. Their house. But . . . Poppy? And Mason? My new family? Sort of family. Could anybody really be my family? Monnie was my family.

"You'll come?" he said.

I couldn't even whisper yes. I just nodded.

Poppy tucked his beard into his pants, then hitched up his pants some. "Good," he said. "I painted up your room real good. Green paint. Left over from the porch."

I felt my throat go tight, and I found myself blinking back tears. Again! But still I couldn't find words.

But I guess Poppy is used to people being silent, and he didn't seem to expect an answer. He just looked around a moment, saw Child creeping toward the edge of the porch, then went and scooped her up. He brought her back to me, and before I knew what he was doing, he had plopped her into my lap.

I pulled back. I didn't want her in my lap. Didn't know how to talk to her. Or anything. Didn't want her little hands creeping round my face.

Poppy didn't seem to notice how stiff I got, though. He acted real pleased. Child peered into my face, looking at me hard. Her eyes are a bit filmed over and don't focus quite right, so you can't tell if she's looking at you or looking over your shoulder. But I got a pretty strong feeling that she was looking at me. After a minute of looking like that, she put her forehead against mine, hard against mine, not bumping, just leaning in. Then she made a low, humming kind of sound that went on awhile. I suddenly knew—well, I thought I knew—that she knew what had happened. And she was telling me she was sorry.

I looked up at Poppy.

He nodded.

I turned back to her.

She hummed some more and leaned her head for

just a moment against my chest, then pulled away. And then she slipped from my lap and into her papa's arms.

Oh, Lord.

All day long people came and went. Food got set out and eaten, and finally, dark came down, fast, the way it does on the mountain.

Mason looked at me. "You want company tonight?" she asked.

I shook my head. "Not tonight," I said. "I want to be alone with Monnie."

She just nodded, and then she and Georgie set to work. Tables got cleaned, the floor got swept, and folks began drifting away. When they were all gone, I looked around and saw that someone had set out a single place at the table where I sat across from Monnie, and left food on the plate—the kind of food that won't spoil if it sits there.

It looked sad, though, just that single plate sitting there. Anyways, it was done, and the house emptied out, and doors shut soft. And they were gone. I knew they'd be back come morning light. And it'd be time to bury Monnie.

I went out to the porch then, watched their shapes fade off in the night mist, drifting away, lanterns going like little fireflies. For a long time, I sat out there, watching the night come down. Overhead I couldn't see stars, not yet, just the sky darkening, the cloud shapes racing with the wind.

I put my head back, felt the wind move against my face, ruffling my hair. Off by the grave, some daffodils moved in the night air. Someone had put them there already, so the earth wouldn't look so bare and hard come morning.

The whole mountain seemed to go still then, still and silent. There were no sounds—no calling of frogs, no swallows dipping and diving, not a single mean old owl setting out for his nighttime raid. Even the wind died down, sighed soft in the trees, softer in the grass, then went still. It seemed like the whole mountain was stopping, catching its breath. Thinking about Monnie. Thinking what to do next—and how in the world it could go on about its business without her.

22

By the time light was breaking over the mountain in the morning, folks were already gathered around the house and the yard. Folks from the mountain were there, but town folks, too—Dr. Harkins, and Nathan and Alice, the Alley people. Word had spread, so Jane probably knew. But I knew she'd not be here, wouldn't be allowed to come. I knew, though, that she was thinking about me.

Mountain people don't spend long over burials, and in little more time than it took the sun to climb over the mountain peak, Monnie was laid to rest. Men threw dirt onto her grave, and oh, my heart ached bad when they did that. Reverend Tucker said some prayers. Folks bowed their heads. And it was over.

My throat hurt so bad from holding back tears,

but I had to hold them back, though I didn't know why. Poppy reminded me to come to them when I was ready. Dr. Harkins reminded me about the paper Monnie had signed, that it was in the bank, and he'd go with me when I was ready. That made me easier in my mind. Folks offered to stay, but I just needed them gone. And then, praise the Lord, they were. I watched them go, knew they had things to do.

I knew, too, that I had things to do. Only thing was, Lord Almighty, I just didn't know what.

I went inside then and looked around. Someone had fixed up Monnie's bed and washed the sheets and the quilts. The pillows were fluffed up so nice, it looked like spring washing days. Looking at that bed, I thought about the Craven children all lumped together in bed. I'd see if their papa would come and take this bed to them. Sometime. Not yet.

I wandered about the house then, picking things up, putting them down. I saw Monnie's old hairbrush, still with her hairs in it, and I slid it away, inside her dresser drawer. On the chair, her clothes were laid out, washed and folded like she might show up and step into them any minute. Under the chair, her house slippers were laid side by side, all stretched out, the way they'd gotten to be from her feet all swollen up. It seemed odd, the clothes and shoes and all—like, what were they doing here without her?

I began touching things then—the chair, table, lamp, books, the table again, plates and cups and spoons. I picked up the quilt from the chair, buried my face in it, smelled Monnie's sweet, powdery smell, and hugged it a moment, then laid it down again.

The fiddle was there alongside her chair where she'd left it last time she'd played, looking lonely, like a forgotten small child. Suddenly I thought—I should have put it in with her, put it in her coffin with her, she'd be missing it. But that was foolish, I knew it was foolish. You couldn't take such things along.

It felt good in my hands, and I held it close to me, the wood so soft, so warm, it felt like a real and living thing, like maybe it was a part of Monnie. I wished I had learned to play it, knew something about it. All I'd learned to do was pluck the strings with my fingers, pick out a tune or two. But I'd never learned that bow, never really learned the fiddle at all. And then I had the thought I'd had before, a few times before—who would play for me now? How could I sing without the fiddle? How could I sing at all without Monnie to play for me? For just a minute, that worried me. But then I realized it didn't matter. I didn't want to sing anyway. Not now.

I went in the kitchen then, and for a long time, I just stood there, thinking. There was so much food. What would I do with all this food? I could bring it with me—to the Boltons. But I didn't know when to go there. It just seemed . . . odd. Would I just walk over there? Would they come for me? What about my things? I mean, I knew they would help out. They're good folks, really, really good folks. Still, there were all these things to decide. And who would help me decide them?

And what about Monnie's things?

After a while, I went to my room, stood in the doorway, looking around. What to take? What to leave? Should I take everything? I'd need my clothes and my books. And Monnie's rocking chair—I had to have that. And her fiddle, of course.

I went in and sat on my bed, looking out the window. The branch was so close, the one that always scratched at my window in the wind. I'd miss that branch. Even maybe miss the old owl who came and hooted from there.

I wondered if I could come back here sometimes. Maybe I could just stay here by myself, maybe on a weekend or something. And maybe, when Jane got back home on the mountain with her brothers and her pa, maybe she would come visit me here, just like she used to. Of course, I guess she could visit at the Boltons', too. But it wouldn't be the same.

Suddenly my throat felt so tight again I could hardly swallow. I got up then, meaning to start packing. But then I sat right back down. Maybe later.

All that day long, I did the same thing—started to do something, then stopped. Started and stopped. I mostly wandered, picking things up, putting them down. Eventually I went and ate a little bit of beans and bread—and then I remembered something: Monnie asked if there'd be beans where she was going! Were there, I wondered? Did she have beans and grits like she wanted? Oh, I hoped she did.

And music.

Through the windows, I could see the sun dipping below the mountain, could feel the night dropping around the house. The wind was picking up, whistling softly through the trees.

I went outside then and sat on the steps, looking around me at the mountain soaring gently upward, the night lying thick up there, the top of one peak hidden in the soft gray of a cloud. I knew it was raining way up there, but here, there was just the moonlight. Somewhere, on the far side of the valley, I heard a coyote call, plaintive and lonely— like a baby's cry, Monnie always said—and it was answered by another nearby.

Swallows were diving, snatching up mosquitoes and bugs, thousands and millions of bugs each night, if Monnie was right about their appetite. And there were bats, too. Monnie hated bats. I don't mind them. They're sweet little creatures as long as you don't mess with them too much.

After a while, deer began coming from the woods into the meadow, their legs looking just like skinny tree trunks. They'd stay free till dawn, and then they'd hide themselves again.

I closed my eyes and laid my head against the porch post, trying not to feel the empty place inside my heart. For a long time I sat there, aching, longing, wanting her, wanting her so bad. Would I ever not want her?

In the sweet by and by, we will meet on that beautiful shore.

I opened my eyes, startled. I'd heard the words so clearly, as if Monnie were right there, as if she had spoken to me. I turned, looking for her, though I knew that was plain foolish. I saw the stars shining so hard and cold, so close to earth, they were almost touching her grave. I looked all around—but of course she wasn't there.

Yet I had heard her voice. I knew I had.

And then I heard her again. And this time, I heard the fiddle, too.

In the sweet by and by, when the angels sing . . .

The wind picked up then, a soft rustling and murmuring, as if the trees themselves were humming. Tears rushed up to my eyes. "Monnie?" I whispered. "Monnie, is that you?"

Again the song came, almost unbearable in its sweetness.

In the sweet by and by, we will meet again. . . .

I swallowed down the bones in my throat. Lord, how could I do this without her? How could I have music without her? "Monnie, no!" I whispered. "Monnie, I can't anymore. I told you that time. Remember?"

And just like that, I heard her laugh, remembered it as clearly as if she was laughing right now, that whooping kind of laughter that sometimes made me mad. And her words that night: 'Course you'll make music, girl. 'Course you'll sing. How could you not?

And then she was gone. I knew she was gone. I no longer heard her, felt her. It was as if her spirit had drifted right off on the breeze. And the only sound left was the wind whispering in the trees—that, and her words, still running round in my head: 'Course you'll sing, girl. How could you not?

I stood up then and looked out toward her grave. "Monnie?" I said.

Nothing.

I stood for another minute, hoping to hear her again. Then I turned and started into the house. At the door, though, I stopped and looked out toward her grave again, feeling a bit—mad, maybe. Monnie always had to have the last word. Even dead, she needed the last word.

Yet in spite of myself, suddenly I felt something welling up. A song, a song was swelling inside of me, throbbing in my throat, pounding in my chest, longing to be let out—and I did, I hummed it, just a few bars:

In the sweet by and by . . . we will meet on that beautiful shore. . . .

And somewhere, somewhere nearby—in the trees, in the wind—in my heart—I heard Monnie humming along with me.

PATRICIA HERMES's

own experiences were the inspiration for a novel in which music is central to the lives of her main characters. Growing up, she writes, "someone was always at the piano, being accompanied by someone on a fiddle, a guitar, a saxophone, a banjo, a ukulele. There were also nights when my father would play a comb. There were even drums on wash pails and someone strumming a washboard." Music was the first connection she made with the people when she visited the mountains of Tennessee, where SWEET BY AND BY is set.

Patricia Hermes is the author of many books for young people, including MAMA, LET'S DANCE. She lives in Fairfield, Connecticut.